LEE WAS FASTEST TO MOVE

Hearing his sister's voice, he looked immediately to the row of phone booths in the shadows under the second-floor balcony. He leveled the Uzi, set on auto, and pulled the trigger.

The magazine emptied before he'd got halfway along the row, and the kick took the bullets higher and higher. Glass, plastic and metal exploded everywhere. A man burst out of one of the untouched booths, firing from the hip. Dave instantly saw that it wasn't Sheever, and he steadied his Linebaugh, waiting for the giant to make his move.

His machine pistol empty, Lee was fumbling for his pistol. Sheever's man saw him and turned toward the helpless boy. Then Zera snapped off a round from the scattergun, but it went wide and high, smashing glass above the man's head.

Dave started to change his aim, and Sheever took that second to make his own move. The Linebaugh hesitated for a single fatal moment....

James McPhee

SURViVAL 2000

FROZEN FIRE

A GOLD EAGLE BOOK FROM
W RLDWIDE.

TORONTO · NEW YORK · LONDON · PARIS
AMSTERDAM · STOCKHOLM · HAMBURG
ATHENS · MILAN · TOKYO · SYDNEY

This one is for Eva Hicks who holds my
hand from far across the sea. With my
appreciation for her enthusiasm and my
thanks for all of her help.

First edition October 1991

ISBN 0-373-63203-7

FROZEN FIRE

"When murderous violence is directed at a member of a family, then the resulting feud will be revenge upon revenge, anger on anger, treachery on treachery and blood on blood."

—*Hard Is the Fortune* by
Chuck Starkwether, 1987

PROLOGUE

"Oh come, all ye faithful,
Joyful and triumphant,
O come ye, O come ye, to Bethlehem."

The faces of the two girls were only inches apart, eyes locked together. Their voices mingled into the merest whisper that hardly disturbed the freezing air inside the patched little tent. Their breath came feathering out in white frost that mingled and hung between them.

"Come and behold him,
Born the King of Angels,"

Ellie Rand put her finger to her lips to warn her younger sister not to let rip on the chorus, knowing what would happen if Sheever heard them singing the carol. It would be bad for Roxanne to encounter the wrath of the blond giant, but worse, so much worse, for Ellie.

"O come, let us adore him,
O come, let us adore him,

O come, let us adore him, Christ the Lord."

Ellie licked her lips. "Shall we do the second verse now?"

"No. I don't like the second verse. When I was at school, Miss Hirschfeld always made us sing that one and we used to giggle and get in loads of trouble with her."

"Why?"

Roxanne lowered her head, the bright green eyes hooded from her sister. "Well, 'cause it's got the words about the virgin's womb in it."

"Well, we could just do the last verse. You know that one?"

Roxanne looked up again. "Sure, let's do that. Except..."

Ellie brushed an errant strand of long black hair from across her face, squeezing her sister's hand. "I know. But we said we'd try not to talk about it so much."

"I know, Ellie. But it *was* Dad, wasn't it?"

The older girl didn't reply immediately. Both of them allowed their memories to go wandering back in time. Back for more than two months. To when the air still held a sweet memory of the lost fall.

It seemed that they'd been riding with Sheever and his gang of psychopathic butchers for ever and ever. In fact, it couldn't have been more than four or five months. Time blurred and memory became shifting and unreliable. There'd been the first days up at their grandmother's home in Montana, before the asteroid devastation struck the earth and changed everything for always. Their father and brothers had been camping down in New Mexico, and the girls still cherished the hope that their father would come after them and find them, no matter where they were.

Society crumbled and millions died. But in the safe north they'd been all right, with their mother to guard them. Then Sheever had come to town with his granite face and his milk-white stallion. And Janine Rand hadn't been able to look after her two daughters quite as carefully as before.

When the gang left, they took Ellie and Roxanne with them. But their mother remained behind, buried in the cold earth.

"I heard Melmoth barking. I'm sure I did," insisted Roxanne.

Ellie patted her arm. "I thought I heard *some* dog barking, as well. Just before the mountain sort of fell down on top of everything."

"It was Melmoth—I know it was!"

The older girl sighed. "I was sure it was, and we both saw Lee that time in camp. But why haven't they rescued us? Have they given up?"

"No."

"Shh. Keep your voice down. If Sheever ever finds out that it was Dad and Lee trailing after us...I don't know what he'd do."

"There was somebody else with them, wasn't there? First the black doctor that..." There was a silence as they remembered the black doctor and what had happened to him at Sheever's hands. Lifted into the air, strangled, his neck snapped. "And the woman by the mountain. But by the river, it looked like there was another woman with them. Didn't it?"

"Yeah... We've already talked this over so much, haven't we?"

"I guess so. I think Dad's dead, and that's why he won't..."

The light of the bright fire outside their tent barely shone through, but it was enough for Ellie to see the tiny pearl of moisture trickling from her sister's right eye, down the cheek.

"Let's sing that last verse of the carol, and then we can go to sleep. I'm certain Dad and Lee aren't far from us, Roxanne."

"Honest?"

"Honest."

"When *is* Christmas?"

Ellie smiled. "Don't know. Lemuel said he didn't know either, but he said—" she paused for a second to adopt the man's tight Southern voice "—'fucking soon, less'n I miss my guess, girly. Coupla weeks, mebbe.' ''

Roxanne wiped her tears away. ''Last verse, then. Real quiet.''

''Yea, Lord, we greet thee,
Born this happy morning,
Jesus to thee be glory given,
Word of the Father,
Now in flesh appearing.''

They both put fingers to lips and giggled, just like two sisters sharing a secret joke together in their bedroom when the parents have left them.

''O come, let us adore him,
O come, let us adore him,
O come, let us adore him, Christ the Lord.''

A FEW PACES from the tent, stretched out to his full seven feet, Sheever lay by the fire, scraping at his nails with a thin-bladed flensing knife. They'd camped for three nights in the same place, resting the animals. The horses and one surviving pack mule were in poor shape, finding it hard to forage in the remorseless grip of iron winter. It had meant ditching some of their weapons, including all but one of their machine guns and mortars.

They'd been discussing the problem of supplies that evening. Now Sheever turned to his main lieutenant and laughed. "Perhaps we shall obtain all we want as Christmas presents, eh?"

1

Melmoth rolled onto his back, offering his belly to be rubbed. The pit bull was thin, ribs showing, but his spirits were still high. Particularly now they'd found somewhere out of the biting easterly that had been blowing for the past three days.

Zera leaned over and obliged the brindled crossbreed, scratching his chest, up under the long jaw. "Boy, this is the life, Melmoth," she said.

"Want me to get some more wood for the fire, Dad?" Lee Rand asked.

"No. Rest up. I'll get some when we need it. Fire's good right now."

Dave Rand stood up and looked out of the cabin window. There was a thick crust of snow, leaving only one half of one of the top panes clear. The sky was still the familiar leaden gray, clouds seeming to press down on the very tops of the forest around them. Light was failing, and night would soon be shedding its dark pools of shadow around them. It hadn't snowed since the previous evening, but the depth against the wall of the wooden hut was well over six feet. Out on the open trail it lay over a foot thick, making walking difficult and tiring.

"Dark yet?" Lee prompted.

"Soon. I'll go get some wood for the night in a couple of minutes."

"I can go, Dave," offered the young woman, sitting back on her heels, ignoring Melmoth's plaintive whine at her neglect.

"No."

He looked around the cabin. They'd been lucky to find it, although the long months of wilderness survival living had honed Dave's skills to the point where luck didn't come into it so much. He'd seen the small township in the valley far below them and the honeycomb of trails snaking through the hills. He'd guessed there'd be some isolated homes off side trails.

They weren't the first there.

The door had been jimmied open, springing a padlock, and the food store had been raided. But the structure was still solid, giving protection against the harsh winter, and the hearth was big enough for a roaring fire of dry branches.

"How long till Christmas, Dad?"

"I think it's December 9 today." Dave's training as an accountant had given him the gift of accuracy. It was the ninth day of December, in the year of our Lord, 2050.

"Think we're close to Sheever?" said Zera, joining Dave by the window.

"Word we keep hearing is that we're closing in on him again."

It wasn't just what they heard.

Sheever and his gang of deserters left a number of human signposts to mark their passing. Corpses, mostly female, all mutilated.

In the past few days the bodies had been more recently killed, some hardly touched by predators.

Lee coughed and his father immediately moved to him. "You okay?"

The boy laughed. "Sure. Just because I was double-sick for a few days, you think I'm going to die every time I sneeze."

"It wasn't a few days, Lee," said Dave. "And it was more than double-sick."

THE ILLNESS HAD STARTED only a day or so after the volcanic cataclysm that had taken the life of their other traveling companion, Kate Mazursky. At that point they'd been less than a mile behind Sheever, but the weather had been appalling and they were on foot and the gang was mounted.

On the third of those grindingly hard days, Lee had started to cough.

It had begun as a dry, light cough, as though he were being bothered by dust. But it was unrelievedly cold and muddy. The next night they camped in the open, hungry and bone chilled. By dawn the cough had deepened and loosened up, rattling in his chest. Lee complained that his eyes were sore and it hurt him to take a very full breath.

During the westward slog the next day, his condition grew rapidly worse. Twice he slipped and fell on level ground, and the second time he lay still in the dirt, unable to stop coughing.

Dave remembered that moment like a frozen photograph. He'd stooped by his son and removed the glove from his right hand, touching the boy's forehead. He was unable to hide his own shock at the fiery heat that scorched his fingers.

They'd been close to an abandoned tourist cabin complex. Most of the trim buildings had been wrecked in the search for food and for firewood, but a couple were barely habitable.

It had been ten days before Lee was well enough for them to even consider moving on.

Dave wondered how he could have managed if Zera hadn't been there, and he decided that he couldn't have. Most days he had to be away for long hours, painstakingly tracking down game with the Sauer 120 Lux rifle. Finally he'd centered the Leupold optical sight on a straggler from a herd of goats. A lame kid, its flank covered in barely healed claw scars. As Dave had heaved it up on his shoulders, he'd wondered about the predator that had caused those wounds, and guessed it could only be a fair-sized grizzly.

By the time he'd returned, Lee had been through the crisis of the fever and was sleeping easily, his face beaded with sweat. There was a swollen bruise on his right cheek and a smear of dried blood from his nose.

Zera had looked exhausted. "Bad times here, lover," she'd said to him, giving him what started as a casual kiss on the cheek and turned into a full-fledged embrace. "Lee freaked late morning. Knocked me down and kicked Melmoth. Started off walking into the snow, ball naked. I brought him back. Melmoth didn't know which way was up."

Though the sickness had burned itself out, it had fretted Lee's body close to the point of no return. He hadn't eaten properly for a week, and his ribs stood out against the pallor of his body. Dave feared that if he touched his son, the bones would crack through the parchment skin.

But the mountain had been climbed, and there remained the slow descent down the other side. Zera had cooked up a wonderful rich stew from the goat, which she'd complemented with herbs she found in the woods. Dave then shot a second of the herd, this time a tough, stringy old-timer. But the young woman had made even that into a succulent broth, filled with tender shreds of light meat.

Lee was all for starting off again three days after that, insisting that he was feeling fine and ready to go after Sheever. Unfortunately he stumbled and went flat on his face on the dirt floor of the cabin and weakened his case a little.

Even when they finally did start off again on the vengeance trail, Lee was in a desperately weakened state. It was all he could do to cover three miles by late afternoon, with frequent stops.

But each day saw him stronger and fitter, striding out ahead of Zera and his father, running and laughing with the excited Melmoth.

The only question remaining in Dave Rand's mind was where his prey was moving. Initially he knew that Sheever's destination had been a box canyon somewhere in Idaho. But now the trail was going south and west, toward the state line with Oregon, or what had once been the state line before Adastreia made things like that irrelevant.

"THINK I MIGHT GO hunting tonight," Dave said, wiping away at the window and trying to peer out.

"What about those bear tracks we saw yesterday?" Lee said. "Best I come with you?"

"Could all go?" Zera offered.

"A man alone has the edge. I'll wait and see what kind of moon there is. Take Melmoth with me. He's getting better and better as a tracker."

They were low on food. Twice Dave had missed long shots, once at a deer and once at what he thought was probably an elk, but he never saw it clearly enough through a snow flurry to be sure.

"Bring me a pineapple-and-ham pizza with double olives," said Lee.

Zera grinned. "I'll settle for a triple eggburger with strawberry shake and extra fries. And Melmoth'll go big on a plate of fried chicken breasts with beef gravy."

Dave nodded. Putting on a flat, droning voice, he gazed up at the ceiling. "Hi, I'm Dave and I'll be assisting Sprite in serving you today."

"Sprite!" exclaimed Lee. "Come on, Dad."

"No. We were up Monarch Pass, before you and the girls came along, and there was a waitress there called Sprite. She was assisting this huge giant called Randy. Mom and I could hardly keep our faces straight."

"I worked in a vacation resort hotel once," said Zera, assuming the same sort of expression and voice as Dave. "I'm Zera and I'd like to tell you all about tonight's special entrée. The chef has selected a boneless breast of chicken and palpitated it with a light cranberry sauce, marinating it in a frost of freeze-whipped lima beans. He offers it for your dining pleasure on a bed of spinach, fresh as tomorrow's sunrise, and handpicked creamed okra."

Dave and Lee applauded her, and the noise made Melmoth leap eagerly to his feet, thinking there was going to be some action.

"All right, boy," said Dave. "Let's go see what the outdoor eatery has to offer tonight." He flashed a grin at Zera. "Hand-shot for your dining pleasure."

IT WAS A GOOD hunter's moon, but the low cloud meant that its brightness was often veiled.

Dave had the huge .475 Linebaugh handgun tucked in its holster on his belt, and a rifle across his shoulder. The ten-inch Trailmaster knife was sheathed on his left hip. Apart from the double layer of thermal underclothes, he also had on a shirt and sweater under the quilted anorak. Though the cold was intense, Dave kept the hood down, knowing that awareness of the surroundings was more important than having warm ears.

Melmoth panted eagerly at his heels, burrowing through the deeper patches of snow like a small but immensely powerful engine.

Dave's boots crunched through the iced crust, leaving a clear trail behind him. The trees were layered with snow, and he had to keep ducking to avoid showering himself. There was a stream, mostly frozen, a quarter mile from the cabin, and he made for it, guessing that it was the most likely place to come across any game.

The nearer he got, the more cautious he became, setting down each step with measured care. He knelt to pat Melmoth, whispering to gentle the pit bull so that he didn't get overexcited.

The dog suddenly stiffened, a snarl beginning deep in his throat. It wasn't the usual early warning of something moving in the vicinity. This was something special, and it raised the hairs at the nape of the man's neck.

"Quiet," he said, his voice hardly audible even to himself.

But Melmoth was showing every sign that he was about to go crazy. His legs were trembling, and a worm of clotted saliva was dangling from the parted jaws. The long, low snarl was rumbling on and on.

Moving with infinite caution, Dave unslung the rifle, readying it. Turning his head slowly from side to side, he peered into the great blocks of blinding shadows.

Now he could feel it.

He opened his mouth and breathed in slowly, tasting the air on the back of his tongue. There was something there. A bitter, rutting sort of scent that lay heavy on his palate.

He had the feeling that he was being watched. There was an overwhelming temptation to turn and run. Run away from whatever it was that was waiting and watching in the trees.

"No," he said quietly. His finger was on the trigger of the rifle, taking up the first pressure.

One of his survival instructors back in California had warned of panic. "Run scared, and you can run smack into whatever is scaring you."

He crouched and tried to peer toward the narrow river, trying to determine if there was a chunk of deeper blackness down there.

The bushes ahead stirred, and he heard ice crackle and snap. It was a thin, musical sound like glass breaking among the pines.

Melmoth took a couple of uncertain steps forward, then stopped, turning his head back to Dave, wanting reassurance from his master.

There was a faint snuffling sound, like a hog tearing at a carcass, and Dave caught a pluming trail of white breath. But he still couldn't make out what it was a few yards below him.

At that moment the shrouded moon vanished behind a bank of thicker cloud, driven from the east. The half light changed abruptly to no light at all.

He remained motionless, rifle ready, waiting. The wind was gusting, and it came rattling down the valley, loosening snow from heavy branches, sending it cascading to the ground in a flurry of soft sound.

It also cleared the clouds, and light flooded back into the open spaces between the towering pines.

The creature by the river was on the move, padding fast up the slope toward the man and dog, more quickly and quietly than anything that size should have been capable of.

Even in the shadows Dave had no difficulty in recognizing it as a massive grizzly, jaws open, rank breath preceding it.

He stood and spun around, ready to either move fast or shoot, whichever was the better option.

But he found himself a mere yard away from a second bear, reared on its hind legs, ten feet tall.

One casual smash of its front paw knocked the rifle spinning from his hands.

"Shit," he said.

2

Dave Rand knew a little about the great North American grizzly bear. *Ursus horribilis,* to give it the proper scientific name. Vastly muscled, toweringly tall, the grizzly is to the land what the great white shark is to the seas. It can run much faster than a man over a short distance. It can run much faster than a man over a long distance. It can swim, and when younger, can climb trees with amazing agility. It doesn't have particularly good sight; then again, neither does the great white.

Manuals for backpackers and survivalists are filled with advice on how to react when a grizzly is encountered on the trail. Sadly much of that advice is contradictory and often ends up with a sentence that generally begins: "If all of this fails . . ."

Dave knew that most fatal attacks involved bears going after campers' food, or situations where a human literally bumped into an unsuspecting grizzly on a blind trail in the high country.

Some remembered advice floated back into his consciousness. "Don't make a noise, assume a submissive posture, and walk slowly backward until at a safe distance. Then turn and move briskly in the opposite direction.''

Dave had always liked that bit. *Briskly.*

He'd asked his instructor what steps to take if confronted with a grizzly.

"Fucking long ones," she'd replied.

Nothing he'd ever read or heard told him what to do when caught between *two* grizzlies.

Dave always found that his mind performed oddly in conditions of great stress. As he stumbled away from the nearer bear, his first concern was that his bladder had involuntarily relaxed. Hot liquid flooded down the legs of his pants.

The next minute or so seemed to last an eternity of action and noise and violence, and at no time did he have the least sensation of control. It was just a series of sliced vid-pix, each one a splinter of frozen time.

As the slashing paw ripped the rifle from his hands, he pulled on the trigger. There was the crack of the explosion, flat and dulled in the open among the snow-covered trees. But it was loud enough to startle the grizzly, and the beast checked its follow-up lunge at the man. The claws, eight inches long, hissed through the air only a touch away from Dave's face as he began to move away. The stink of the huge creature was overpowering, making him gag.

Melmoth went berserk.

Driven stone-crazy by the appearance of the two bears, the pit bull had leapt into a fighting mania. He charged straight at the nearer animal, then locked powerful jaws on the hind leg, just above the ankle. Dave heard with a strange clarity the crack of bone under the impact of the dog's teeth. The grizzly threw its head back and roared in pain and shock, its bared fangs gleaming like silvered ivory in the moonlight.

It reached down and swiped at Melmoth like a child swatting away an irritating hornet. But a full-grown pit bull doesn't swat away that easily, and the bear had to swing twice more, clumsily stooping, before it made contact.

Once again Dave heard the sickening sound of bone snapping, but this time it was Melmoth who went howling into a snowbank, rolling over and over.

The grizzly was still reared up on its hind legs, head weaving from side to side, eyes glowing like live coals in the darkness. Behind it Dave was vaguely aware that the second grizzly, the ponderous hump of muscle and fat marking it as a sow, was looming up the slope from the stream.

He fumbled for the butt of the Linebaugh, the gloves making him clumsy. Stark fear made him even slower. It seemed as though years passed by and dust gathered on his shoulders before the massive pistol came free from the greased holster.

Melmoth, shaking his head and staggering, was ready for a second round. Dave noticed there was blood streaming down his flanks, raven black in the moonlight.

"No, boy!" he shouted, trying to save the dog's life. But the pit bull was red-eyed blind, and nothing would keep him from the massive enemy except the intervention of death itself.

The shout decided the grizzly between the small four-legged attacker and the bigger, two-legged one. It swayed in Dave's direction, unsheathed claws slashing toward him.

He braced his right wrist with his left hand, leveling the single-action, static-breech revolver at the beast.

The blued eight-inch barrel gaped at the throat of the grizzly. Dave took a gulp of breath and squeezed the trigger.

He cocked and fired a second time, the kick running clear up to his shoulder, rocking him on the frozen snow.

"Bastard!" he hissed.

The light wasn't good enough to make out the results of the two huge rounds. But he knew that he must have blown holes bigger than the span of his hand out of the bear's back.

The grizzly lurched, taking two steps sideways, blood suddenly frothing from its muzzle and jaws,

streaking the silver-gray fur of its chest. Rank breath
plumed whitely from its mouth as it bellowed, a
deafening roar that made Dave's head ring.

The Linebaugh held only five rounds of .475 full-
metal-jacket ammo, which should have been enough
to neutralize a full-grown elephant. But Dave Rand
now faced a terminal dilemma. Two rounds gone,
and the nearest of the bears still standing. Hit hard,
but still menacing. And the sow was nearly on him.
Three rounds left in the handgun. Put one more in
the towering male, and that only left two for the sow.

Melmoth was growling at the second of the grizzlies, snapping at its legs and distracting it for a few
vital seconds.

Dave backed cautiously away, eyes raking the
ground beneath the trees for the discarded rifle. Finally he spotted it lying twenty paces away. Even at
that distance and in poor light, it was obvious that
the stock was smashed to splinters.

The nearest bear dropped to all fours, head shaking, splattering blood and saliva over its chest. The
roaring was quieter, less aggressive. Dave still held
the revolver, the heavy Ruger Bisley Blackhawk
frame perfectly balanced.

"Come on," he mouthed.

There was a yelp of pain from Melmoth as the
other grizzly caught him a glancing blow and sent
him spinning into another drift, where he vanished

completely. Dave watched for several seconds, but the pit bull didn't reappear.

The triple tableau didn't move. The man, braced, with the pistol ready. The first bear, coughing, head down, with its mate at its side, nuzzling it.

"Come on," repeated Dave. "Fucking come on."

Without any warning, the lines all went down at once for the wounded grizzly. Its eyes rolled, white in the pale sheen of the clouded moon, and it pitched forward on its front. The claws dug great rasping gouges in the packed snow, then it was still.

The narrow clearing was almost silent, just the sighing breath of the she-bear and the shallow panting of the man. There was still no sign of life from the shadowed snowbank.

The sow pushed at the massive corpse with her muzzle, as though she were checking that the male bear wasn't just shamming. Then she reared up on her hind legs, turning her long head from side to side. Dave readied himself, considering putting the grizzly away with his last three bullets.

But something held him back.

Though he'd changed in an infinite variety of ways from the contented accountant and family man that he'd been the previous year, Dave Rand was still conscious of entrenched residual values. He'd been a member of the Sierra Club and a number of ecological and conservation societies. All of them were dedicated to the preservation of endangered species like the grizzly in the high mountains.

Now he'd killed one of them. Fine—it was to save his own life, but that didn't make him feel any better about it. But now he was thinking of blasting a second grizzly off the planet.

He steadied himself and fired two rounds from the Linebaugh, pointing the gun into the midnight sky.

He waited, one last round still in the chamber, under the hammer. He knew that if he needed to shoot one more time, it would have to be a clean killing shot to the head.

The grizzly rocked from side to side, disturbed by the booming sound of the smoking gun. It took a shuffling half step toward Dave, then stopped again. The creature threw its head back and roared out, the echoes bouncing from the mountain slopes around.

Then it turned and dropped from its hind legs to retreat in a fast, rolling gait. Dave watched it carefully until it disappeared into the impenetrable blackness beyond the stream. He stood and listened, hearing its lumbering progress through the snowy brush, and then the forest was filled only with a great stillness.

Fingers trembling a little, Dave reloaded the handgun and holstered it. He glanced once at the wrecked rifle and left it where it had fallen. Before moving to the shadow-speckled drift, he paused by the mighty carcass of the male grizzly.

"Sorry," he said.

ZERA WIPED HER SLEEVE across the condensation on the inside of the glass, trying to see out. Lee was sleeping in front of the fire, tossing uneasily. She'd laid her palm on his forehead and had found it was hot. Not as bad as when the fever had first appeared, but still way up.

"Come on, Dave," she said, pressing her face against the cool glass. The memories of the way the boy had fought and thrashed when delirium overtook him were still painfully fresh. Now, if it was returning...

Dave had been gone for well over an hour and a half. Close on two hours. Once she'd thought she'd caught the faint sound of gunfire, but it hadn't been repeated and the rising wind rode over everything.

"Getting cabin fever," Zera whispered. Only ten minutes ago she'd looked out over the snowy ground and had thought she'd spotted someone moving.

The really odd thing was that it had looked like a ghostly monk. A cowled figure, floating slowly between the trees, illuminated by the broken spears of moonlight, then disappearing again.

"Goin' t'beat the fucking critical total on the next fuckin' round."

She sighed, looking back at the muttering figure. Lee's face appeared ruddy in the fire's glow, and she could see the sheen of sweat on his temples and cheeks. His hands plucked at his shirt, as though he were trying to attract his own attention.

Far off, like a dream heard through muffling layers of muslin, the young woman caught the noise of a dog barking. Just once, faint and weak.

"Melmoth," she said.

Dave Rand appeared ten minutes later, trudging slowly toward the cabin, boots kicking up spurts of powdery snow, breath hanging around his mouth. There was enough light for Zera to see that he was carrying something. She at first assumed he was bringing game, and only when she opened the door of the hut to him did she realize that Dave was carrying Melmoth, cradled in his arms.

"I got good news and I got bad news," he said to her, laying the wounded animal on the dirt floor of the cabin.

"Me, I just got bad news," replied Zera.

3

Dave climbed out of his clothes, and used the water heating over the fire to try to wash out the blood and urine.

Zera took the injured Melmoth, laying him gently on a nest of torn blankets in front of the brightly burning wood. She probed carefully at him while Dave undressed, trying to find out how bad the wounds were by judging the pit bull's reactions. But he seemed to realize that the young woman was trying to help him and only snarled a little when she touched his right side.

"Rib's gone," she reported. "Two or three. I think his shoulder's been dislocated...it's real tender there, but it looks like it went straight back in again. Some superficial cuts and grazes."

Dave pulled on his wet pants; none of them now carried much in the way of spare clothing. Standing by the fire, he was surrounded by a rising halo of steam. "How 'bout his ear? That's where most of the blood seemed to be coming from."

Zera shook her head, straightening. "Should call him Van Gogh instead of Melmoth. The right ear's been torn clean off."

"Stitch it?"

"No. Not worth it. Cold like this should help heal it. Keep an eye on it for infection. Ribs are a lot more serious."

"Best bind him up."

"Sure. I'll do it. How about Lee?"

Dave had looked at his son immediately when Zera told him about the revival of the feverish illness. But the boy had been sleeping fitfully. Now his father came back to him again.

"Don't know. Seemed like a strep throat to start with. Then that virus got its teeth in him. But I thought it had all burned itself out."

"What can we do?"

"First light, I'll go and cut some meat off the dead grizzly—if the wolves or whatever haven't gotten there first. Should keep us going for days."

"Going?"

"Yeah."

Zera moved to stand by him, her voice showing her bewilderment. "Dave? What does 'going' mean? Where are we going and when are we going?"

"Look . . . we've been closing in on Sheever, making up for the lost time. Can't slow down now. Lee'll be fine."

"No, he won't."

"What?"

Zera grabbed him and shook him hard, making his teeth rattle. "Listen to me, Dave! You're getting crazed on this hunt."

"But the girls are..."

"Fuck that!"

"They'll be going through hell with..."

Zera still gripped him tightly. "Your brain's falling apart, lover. Ellie and Roxanne are going through what they've been going through for months. I'm not saying that's anything but double-shitty. But you can't sacrifice everything else to try and rescue them. Lee is fucking ill!"

The eyes had been staring through her to the rough, clay-filled logs of the cabin walls. Now they cleared and he looked straight at Zera. At last he nodded.

"Sorry, love. You're right. Get Lee well again and then we can move."

"Right," she said.

By LATE the following morning, Lee had slipped into a sort of coma. To try to cool him down, they'd damped the fire and rolled him in rags they'd wet with snow. But the teenager was so fiery hot that Dave almost expected to see his son's skin hiss as the moisture touched him.

Melmoth, by contrast, was markedly better, even managing to totter off his own rumpled bed and stagger across to poke his nose toward his sick young master. But Lee was sunk deep into his own nightmare world of scorching darkness.

He kept turning uncomfortably, hands fluttering toward his face. Though Dave listened carefully, he could catch no more than an odd word here and there from the monotone mumbling that dribbled occasionally from his son's lips.

There was anxiety in the muttering. Lee seemed to be wandering through some blank wilderness tainted with blasphemous entities that gibbered and clawed at him, preventing him from sustaining a quest.

Dave sat on the floor and held Lee's hand, trying to calm his son. He felt the raging heat that raced through the boy, sucking at the core of his life.

Dawn had brought a fresh blizzard from the north. Ice layered the inside of the window, and new-fallen snow piled against the door. They had enough wood to keep a fire burning in the hearth for at least another forty-eight hours, but they were running perilously low on food.

"Can't go out and get meat from the bear," Dave said, scratching at the ice with his nail and peering into the leaden afternoon. "Not in this. Have to wait for it to ease." He turned to Zera. "Still . . . least it'll be holding Sheever, as well."

The snow began to fade away around four in the afternoon, but it was replaced by a demonic thunderstorm that roiled around the mountains until well past dusk. The temperature rose by at least twenty degrees, and rain pelted down. The snow turned into gray hills of slush that slithered away, the tracks becoming rivers of seething mud.

Lightning turned night into electric-brilliant day, and Dave considered going out in the storm after meat. But the air was filled with the stench of ozone, and it was almost impossible to speak above the thunder.

Lee slept.

Once he woke and sat up, hair pasted lankly to his narrow skull. "Dad, can I go down the store to get a soda?"

"What?"

Lee turned his head, eyes glowing in their sockets like the hobs of hell. His lips parted dryly and he nearly smiled. "We aren't, then we are, and last of all we fucking aren't."

While Dave and Zera stared at him, the boy folded himself back into sleep again.

After midnight, Melmoth mumbling in his sleep, Lee breathing fast and shallow, Zera cat-footed over to where Dave was dozing in his sleeping bag. She knelt naked at his side and touched a finger to his lips.

"Lover," she whispered.

"What's the matter?" The line between darkness and waking is often blurred and confusing. He'd been wandering into a half dream about Janine, his dead wife. They'd been at an aquarium, walking through silent green corridors, unspeaking, separate.

She touched her finger again to his mouth, teasing the sensitive skin. Heat radiated from her body, and a heady, musky scent clung to her.

"Know what I'm thinking of? Know what I'd like right now?"

"Yes. Yes to both the questions. And I'm real sorry, Zera, but the answer is no to the next question."

"Why?" She squatted back on her heels. The storm had moved on, and the small window gave enough moonlight so he could see her. The stark line of her shoulders, softening to her breasts, dark tipped. Down over the flat muscular wall of her stomach and the V of curling blond hair that sprang from her parted thighs.

"Come on..."

"What's that mean?"

"It means I don't want to make love to you, Zera. Not now."

She sniffed and half turned away from him. "You sure, lover? Can't you be persuaded...?" She reached for him through the soft material of the sleeping bag.

"I'm sure. Just...too much of everything. I'm sorry, love."

Then she laughed, and the tension eased. "All right, old-timer. Guess it'll be up to me to please myself tonight. But tomorrow..."

IF ANYTHING, Lee was a fraction worse in the morning. His forehead wasn't burning up, and he was able to sip at a mug of melted water, held by Zera. But he kept slipping into a deeper level of unconsciousness. Throughout it his eyes remained closed and his pulse was even more shallow, speeding away like a fading hammer-beat.

Dave stood in the open door of the cabin, taking deep breaths of the moist green air. "Can't believe how the weather keeps changing," he said. "Blizzard one minute, thunderstorm the next, and then along comes a thaw."

"You going for that meat?" the young woman said, laying Lee gently back on his makeshift pillow.

"Sure. Melmoth looks like he might make it all right."

Even as he said it, Dave was conscious that he'd made an unspoken comparison with his own son. Melmoth looked as though *he* were going to make it. He could stand and move stiffly, and the wound where his ear had been seemed healthy.

Lee was visibly worse.

"How long will you be?"

"Hour. Give or take. After so much rain and flooding, I don't know what the tracks'll be like." He glanced up at the sky. "Got a feeling that it could change all over again. Some high thunderheads might bring us some more snow. I'll go right away."

His forecasting was uncannily prescient.

He went out, hefting the scattergun, as well as the reloaded pistol. He also took along a large burlap sack to carry the meat in. Within fifteen minutes the clouds had flowed down off the mountaintops and filled the valley, bringing with them a drop to way below freezing. Every tree and bush was instantly draped in glittering beads of pure ice, like an illustration from a child's book of fairy tales.

The muddy puddles scarring the trail froze in a matter of minutes, making the walk down toward the stream a perilous expedition. His boots slipped, and twice he came close to falling, risking a sprained ankle or a broken wrist.

Dave considered turning and retracing his steps back to the cabin. But he knew that Lee's chances of survival would diminish along with their shrinking food supplies.

Then it began to snow again. A classic whiteout, with the land quickly covered and a driving wind carrying the tiny flakes along parallel to the earth. The horizon disappeared completely, and it became impossible to orientate himself.

Dave reached the point where he thought he'd slaughtered the male grizzly, but there was no sign of the body. The snow had covered any sign of the fight, hiding the ruin of the hunting rifle.

Either the scavengers had been out faster than Dave had guessed, or maybe men had taken the gigantic corpse. Or other bears had dragged away the body.

That was the least comfortable option to consider, and Dave straightened, with his back against a convenient fir tree.

He scouted down as far as the narrow stream. It had been turned by the changes in the weather into a raging torrent fifteen feet wide, carrying torn branches and whole small trees in its foaming jaws.

On the way back up the slope, eyes squinting against the snow, Dave was suddenly aware of a tall shape looming out of the whiteness ahead and above him.

He dived sideways, finger tight on the trigger of the Browning 12-gauge.

A quiet, calm voice said, "Don't shoot me, Brother. Or your ailing son will certainly sleep tonight in the bosom of Abraham."

4

The hand-lettered rectangle of white card pinned to the door of his room read Brother David Alexander Rand.

The one on the room opposite said Brother Zera. The young woman had demonstrated her very mixed feelings at being told that she would be treated like an honorary man during their stay.

Lee was up in the sanatorium, tucked between spotless linen sheets, under the care of Brother Athanasius. His temperature had been brought under control, and he was showing encouraging signs of fighting against the infection. Brother Athanasius had explained to Dave Rand that he'd been using an age-old combination of rare herbs, infused and refined into a sweet potion, to treat the virus. "Combined with some of our shrinking store of antibiotics," he'd added with a grin.

Melmoth had been taken into the rooms in the basement, where Brother Dominic practiced his trade as veterinarian. There the brindled pit bull had been bathed and poulticed, his ribs bandaged and other cuts and grazes covered with ointment. To keep the dog calm during the treatment, Brother Dominic had found it necessary to inject Melmoth with a powerful tranquilizing drug.

"More for my good health than his," joked Brother Dominic.

DAVE SAT on the narrow but comfortable bed and looked around the room. The brothers called it "a cell." It was around ten feet long by eight feet broad, with a low, plastered ceiling. The walls were painted in a uniform pale blue, with no pictures to break the monotony. There was a narrow window on the wall opposite the door, with two vanadium-steel bars set into the stone of the sill. It wasn't possible to see any more than a slim section of the sky.

Apart from the bed, the room held a table that folded from the wall and a cane-backed chair, a cupboard with two shelves and a rail to hang clothes.

From what Dave had seen in the few hours they'd all been there, every cell was more or less the same. The oak door was studded with iron nails. It had no lock.

The cowled figure that had loomed at him from the snow was Brother Thomas. He was a bearded man who told him that they'd been observing the cabin since their arrival and had decided the time had come to intervene in their problems.

He'd also explained something about the reclusive order of which he was a senior member.

"We call ourselves the Brothers of the Sunset Sword. We were founded in the fall of 2048 at the bequest of a very wealthy man from Passaic, New Jersey. His name is forever sacrosanct to us. He believed that the world was ending and that a group of dedicated brothers might help to save it by prayer and contemplation."

"He was right about the world ending," Dave had replied.

"We believe he was right in all things. Our name comes from his profound wish that culture should not wither on the branches of the dark ages to come. So we came here. Only twenty of us, carefully selected. Three have died since then. This building was placed with great wisdom, so that its location would protect it from casual interlopers."

"Nobody's found you up here since the asteroid hit us?"

Brother Thomas had smiled. A thin, bleak smile that failed to reach the dark brown eyes. "Only a very few, Brother David. And they stayed but a short while before being pointed along the one-way street of life."

"You killed them?"

"Let's just say they all settled their account with the Lord's credit card with no balance outstanding."

FOR MEN OF PEACE, the building that served as their headquarters was better armed than the average Hell's Angels base. There was a host of shotguns, rifles and pistols, with a couple of bracket-mounted LMGs and a mortar on the roof. They had also installed a sophisticated defense-and-security system including las-scans and heat sensors.

Brother Thomas showed Dave and Zera around with obvious pride, demonstrating the neat nuke-gen, whirring flawlessly away. "It was also designed to use solar power, but there has been little enough of that in the last year or so."

The supply rooms were fairly well filled, but it was here that Dave began to notice the first cracks in the grand design of the brotherhood.

"Lot of empty shelves in here, Brother Thomas," he commented.

"It was not always so. Every shelf was stocked to bursting point. But with twenty of us... well, seventeen of us... I fear our food is diminishing at an alarming rate."

Zera spotted several lights that were out, and one of the big freezers stood open. She asked Brother Thomas about it.

"I fear you outlanders have a keen eye, Brother Zera," he replied. "Sadly the first of our casualties was Brother Christopher. An accident with a power cable translated him from us. And he was our only

tech-brother. Without him there have been some...
deficiencies appearing."

Despite the deficiencies, the first five days in the
hidden retreat were almost unbearably luxurious.
Hot baths whenever they wanted one, and a range of
food above and beyond anything they'd tasted for
much too long.

There was a good library of books to occupy Dave
Rand, including a couple of novels he'd never read
by one of his favorite writers, Cormac McCarthy.

Zera spent much of the first two days in the vid-
room until a fault developed in the main player and
the screen went terminally blank.

"We haven't used it too much in the last few
months," bespectacled Brother Rufus said apolo-
getically.

"SORRY I'VE BEEN such a double-feeb," said Lee,
sitting up in his sanatorium bed.

"Yeah. I never thought any son of mine would
turn out such a wimp."

Lee sniffed, then grinned. "Wimp! Nothing like
using a real up-to-now phrase, Dad. Wimp. You'll be
saying it's all 'out of sight, man. Cool and groovy.'
That sort of real old stuff."

"I can't wait for you to have some kids and then
sit there while they mock you, Lee."

"That, Dad, will definitely be the day."

Father and son smiled at each other, alone in the bright room. From somewhere below them they caught the faint sound of a dog barking angrily.

"Melmoth getting better," Lee remarked.

"Right."

"I can get up this afternoon. Brother Athanasius said so. So I can go and see Melmoth."

Dave stood and looked out of the slit window. The sky was peach-pink, with clouds of gray, streaked with purple, showing where the storms of the previous night were fading away.

"Melmoth's still weak. He doesn't think he is and behaves like he's ready to go and kick the shit out of another grizzly. The ribs are healing, but he'll never grow another ear."

"How long we goin' to stay here, Dad? I reckon I can be ready for the trail in about another couple of days."

"Make that another seven or eight days."

"But Sheever'll be . . ."

"Fuck Sheever!" said Dave. "He can wait for us. There's some saying about revenge being a dish that's best tasted cold. We can wait."

BROTHER TIMOTHY was the oldest of the group and had once been the abbot of a monastery on the outskirts of San Luis Obispo. He and Brother Thomas were joined with Brother Loren as the triumvirate that ran the isolated retreat. The three of them had invited Dave to join them for an evening meal.

"All right for Lee and Zera to come along, as well?" he'd asked.

Brother Thomas had brought the invitation and he shook his head. "I fear not. Not this time, Brother David."

"Why?"

"Why?"

"Yeah, why can't they come?"

"You might as well ask why your pit bull isn't included in the invitation, Brother David. Surely it's obvious."

"No, Brother Thomas. Oddly enough it isn't fucking obvious at all."

"Pray control your anger, Brother."

"Tell me."

"Brother Lee is, in our eyes, still only the merest child."

"That child has lived through more hardship than all you bunch of introverted lock-ins put together, Brother!"

The man simply nodded. "Perhaps. The girl is . . . well, she is simply a girl."

"We owe you a lot," said Dave. "But that doesn't mean I like many of the rules you got here. Zera's good as most men I ever met. They say courage is just grace under pressure. Well, Zera shows that better than... Still, no point in going on. Like I said...we owe you for treating Lee and for helping the dog. And for the food and shelter."

"That's what we'll be talking about at the meal this evening," said Brother Thomas solemnly. "In the senior dining room at seven."

"I'll be there," Dave replied.

CANNED SALMON with frozen melon was served as appetizer.

It was followed by beef with canned potatoes, peas and carrots for the main course, with some soggy, freshly baked bread. Peach cobbler and pecan ice cream completed the meal.

"A measure of zinfandel, Brother David?" Brother Loren offered, the candlelight twinkling off his gold-rimmed glasses. "It's an excellent wine to go with this food."

"There's an adequate Chablis, if you'd prefer," Brother Timothy suggested. He'd filled his own goblet with the clear white wine, raising it to his lips and sipping. He wiped his silvery beard. "Ah, that really is very good."

"Mind if we talk?" said Dave.

"What about, Brother David?"

"About this meal, Brother Timothy."

"And what do you want to say about the meal, Brother?"

Dave felt his anger rising again. "You ask me here, without either my son or my—" he tried to decide what to call Zera "—my friend."

"Or your dog, Brother David," Brother Loren said with a laugh.

"Or my dog. Now, this is all very nice, but I'd like to get it over with so I can go and rejoin them. You asked me here. Why?"

"To talk, Brother David."

He looked across the polished oak table at Brother Thomas. "I won't play your fucking games."

Brother Timothy raised a hand. "That is enough! Enough!"

He explained in a calm, gentle voice why they had helped Dave and his party in the first place, whereas other travelers had received the shortest of shrifts from them.

"We watched and listened. You seem decent people, and your quest is honorable. And you know how to survive in that fiendish maelstrom of horror out there, beyond these walls."

He pointed with a bony finger to the nearest window, the sleeve of his long gown falling away at the wrist and revealing a platinum Rolex Oyster watch. For some reason Dave found it an irritating display of ostentatious wealth.

"We lack that wisdom. We are men of intellect, and our skills are those of prayer and wisdom."

Dave stood up, the legs of his chair grating on the stone flags of the floor. "I get it. You want someone to do the dirty work for you. Hunting and killing. Jobs that get dried blood down your nails and a callus on the trigger finger."

The older man also stood, face working with anger, his finger now pointing directly at Dave Rand's eyes.

"Impudent cur!"

Dave shook his head and laughed. "How about 'Saracen dog' or 'eat lead, Martian invader'? Don't give me that shit."

"You owe us!" thundered Brother Loren. Now they were all on their feet.

"Fine. We'll pay. I'll go hunt for you tomorrow. I'll hunt for two days and bring you all the game I can get. And Lee and Zera can come with me. They're more use than you crowd of cockless jerk-offs. Two days of hunting and the debt's paid."

"Then what, Brother David?" said Brother Thomas, gesturing to the chairs. "Can we not all sit and discuss this as men of reason?"

"I don't think so." He saw the olive branch and tried to grasp it. "Look...like I said, we're grateful, but we have to move on. We've told you about my daughters and the man Sheever."

"Of course," said Brother Timothy, pasting a rictus of a smile onto his face. "But there is something more than hunting for food."

Dave wasn't really listening. "I'll do better. If you don't get off your asses and hunt for yourselves, then you'll eventually die. This place is already crumbling about your ears. I'll teach a couple of you how to go and find game. How about that? You've got plenty of weapons."

"There is *something more*," repeated Brother Timothy. "We want you to leave the girl behind for us."

5

"What?" Zera demanded, as though she hadn't heard right.

"You stay here."

"Fuck that, Dave!"

"That's what I thought, as well."

Lee joined the conversation. "But why do they want us all to stay, Dad?"

"You and I are to be their hunter-gatherers. Go out in the snow and hurricanes to provide them with fresh meat and fish and berries, while they get on with praying and contemplating."

"And Zera?"

"Brood mare." He deliberately put it as crudely as he could.

The young woman looked at him disbelievingly, jaw dropped, shaking her head. "Come on . . ."

"They mean it. Brother Timothy is serious. So is Brother Thomas and Brother Loren. They don't have much time for women, but they want their closed order to keep going on and on into the future. That means some women to hang around and cook and wash and have plenty of babies."

Zera was silent for several seconds, staring down at the floor. Then she looked up and grinned. "So . . . when do we leave?"

"Soon."

OUTSIDE THE RETREAT the weather had changed for the better. The rain had vanished, and each day was crisp and bright and bitingly cold.

"Good traveling weather," Dave allowed in a low voice.

It was the morning of the second day after his abortive supper with the triple leaders of the Brothers of the Sunset Sword. Since then, he'd been very conscious that they were being watched. It had proved almost impossible to have a conversation with either Zera or Lee without having one of the hooded figures appear around the corner of the corridor.

Brother Thomas had only raised the subject once more, at lunch on the previous day. While stirring his fork around a plate of pasta smothered in tomato sauce, he'd said, idly and casually, "Think about what we discussed, Brother David. Remember that there is a time to reap and a time to sow. A time to live and a time to die. A time to stay and a time to go."

Dave was familiar with the quotation, though he didn't actually remember that last bit of it. But the

threat was as obvious as if the man had held an open
razor against his jugular.

But at last there was a snatched moment with all
three of them together. They stood at an angle of the
pillared cloisters, admiring Melmoth as he strutted
about. It was his first day out of the vet's rooms.

"Yeah," agreed Zera. "So when do we travel?"

"They're charged up about it, so they'll be looking for us to think about making a break."

"Seventeen of them and some double-deadly armaments," Lee said.

"I'll back us three . . . and Melmoth . . . against all
of them. They're thinkers, not doers. They should
wear T-shirts warning that talk is cheap but the price
of action is colossal. We'll do it."

"Someone's coming," said Zera, seeing Melmoth's remaining ear prick up, his head cocked toward a door at the end of the southern passage.

"Talk later." Dave spun on his heel and moved
quickly away.

THE PLAN WAS, of necessity, simple.

Melmoth was allowed to sleep in Lee's cell, which
solved one major problem. With the pit bull leashed,
the boy was to come to Dave's room, where Zera
would also join them.

That part was accomplished the same night, just
after twelve. Zera was last, sliding around the door

noiselessly. "Someone patrolling the corridor," she whispered. "Nearly caught me."

"What if they try to stop us?" Lee asked.

"Don't let them."

The boy looked at his father, face solemn. "Kill them?"

"If we miss this train...might not be another one for a long time."

"Guns?" said Zera.

"Not if there's a better way. If we can get through without killing them, that'll be good. But we do have to get away from here."

"Now?"

"Now, son."

Dave led the way, Lee and Melmoth coming second, with Zera bringing up the rear. She held the nickel-plated Ruger .32 in her right hand. Lee had his own SIG-Sauer 232, while Dave relied on the Trailmaster knife, his Linebaugh and a Skorpion he slung over his shoulder.

The air still held the clinging memory of the supper. Boiled okra and canned ham with corn. Brother Thomas had announced to the group that this was the last of their supply of ham. But that he hoped—he'd cast a sideways glance at Dave Rand—that in the *very* near future they might be obtaining some fresh meat.

Somewhere Dave could hear the sound of music playing. A piano concerto that he thought might be Beethoven, but his classical knowledge was sadly limited. Janine would have known.

"Someone smoking," Lee whispered, catching his father's sleeve.

"Right." Brother Loren was the only one he'd seen smoking, but that didn't mean others might not be doing it at night in the privacy of their own rooms.

The route to the rear exit, their targeted destination, was complicated, involving several turns and twists and going up and down flights of stairs. But most of it was away from the main living accommodation.

The electronic bell in the central tower gave its single chime for the half hour. For security reasons the bell didn't sound outside the retreat, in case it attracted unwelcome interest.

"So far..." Dave started to say in a low voice as he paused at the bottom of the second staircase.

"So good," Brother Thomas answered, flicking on the light switch, revealing himself and five of the brothers, all armed with scatterguns and standing in a semicircle at the top of the stairs.

"Oh, fuck," Zera muttered at the rear, sliding the Ruger quickly behind her back, out of sight of the men above.

"The sort of response I would have expected from a person of the female gender such as yourself, Brother Zera," said Brother Thomas, face wreathed in smiles at the success of his own little trap.

"Shove it up your ass!" Zera yelled, her face contorted with anger.

"Your words can do me scant harm," said Brother Thomas, beginning to descend the narrow steps, the others pressing hard at his heels. There was a moment of jostling confusion.

"You're dead, you smug fucker!" screamed the young woman, pulling the trigger on the handgun.

Immediately the air became filled with the bloody chaos of a close-contact, powder-burn firefight.

Dave had been surprised by the sudden appearance of the half-dozen hooded men, their modern pump-action weapons contrasting oddly with the almost medieval monks' habits. He reacted slowly and badly, cursing himself under his breath for allowing them to get ambushed in such an obvious way.

Then the yell from Zera and the eruption of noise and blood threw him even more.

He took three steps to the side of the stairs, clawing at the Skorpion he had slung across his shoulders. At his elbow Lee was struggling just to hang on to Melmoth, the pit bull dragging at the leash, barking wildly.

The group of men on the stairs were caught by the young woman's fast and total reaction.

Brother Thomas was hit twice in the chest by the first two rounds from the Ruger, dropping his own gun as he toppled forward. As he fell, he left the five remaining brothers exposed to Zera's fire.

One was shot through the lower face, the bullet ripping off most of his jaw and exposing the row of white teeth, the pearly gleam vanishing immediately in a welter of spilled crimson.

A second man was screaming with panic, trying to push a friend in front of him. But Zera's aim was careful, and he fell, blood spouting from a throat wound.

One of them pulled the trigger on his scattergun, and pellets starred into the wall above Lee's head, allowing him to feel the hot noisy breath of their passing.

That was the only shot that any of the men fired.

Not one of them had been ready for this. They had followed Brother Thomas, secure in their numbers and their heavy guns, not for a moment realizing that the trapped trio would retaliate.

And that the dying would begin.

The Skorpion was set on semi-auto. Dave simply balanced himself and kept squeezing the trigger, pumping bursts of 9 mm parabellum into the tangled group on the steep stairs.

Blood and flesh and bone splinters cascaded everywhere. So much blood poured down into the corridor that Lee immediately lost his footing and fell, letting Melmoth off the leash.

Dave felt the machine pistol empty and he dropped it, going for the Linebaugh, aware at the same moment that Zera's Ruger was clicking on the chamber.

A quick glance at the shifting tangle of bodies, dead and dying, showed him that they didn't need any more bullets.

"That's it," he said. "Let's get out of here right now!"

A hand reached and grasped him by the ankle. Dave looked down, Linebaugh leveled, and saw that it wasn't going to be necessary. Brother Thomas was already sliding into eternity, blood pouring from the two wounds in his chest. The eyes were unfocused, like a baby's, and the lips moved slowly.

Dave stopped.

"Why? A man like you...you could have lived here in safety forever. Why?"

"Because failure's no fucking success at all, Brother!"

A single round from the Linebaugh blasted open the lock on the rear door, and they were away into the biting cold of the night.

The moon was veiled, and they moved fast toward the west, Melmoth trotting contentedly behind them. Nearly a quarter of an hour passed before anyone noticed that the pit bull was carrying a severed human hand in his bloodied jaws.

Through the night there was no pursuit, and they felt as though a cloying burden had been lifted from their shoulders.

6

The larders of the retreat had provided them with the chance to stock up on some food to carry with them on the trail. Their packs weighed heavy with cans of soup and stew, strong on protein and vitamins. There were also some chocolate bars to provide them with quick energy as they pushed fast toward the west.

"How're we going to pick up on Sheever, Dad? Could be anywhere after all the delays we've had."

Dave patted Lee on the shoulder. "Weather'll have slowed him some. Those mountains ahead got only one passable highway through it. That's the way he'll have to take. Be some serious snow up there."

They gathered around to peer at the tattered map in Dave Rand's gloved fingers. It fluttered in the light breeze that brought the faint taste of sulphur from some far-off volcanic action.

"We go through that town there, at the foot of the pass," said Zera.

"Called Hope Springs," Lee read from the map.

Dave laughed. "Someone had a nice sense of humor back in Victorian times," he said.

"How's that?"

"Be a hell of a climb up over Faustus Pass."

Zera looked puzzled. "So? I don't get it. Hope Springs, I mean."

"Never heard the saying, 'Hope springs eternal in the human breast,' Zera?"

"No," she said blankly.

Dave smiled. "Oh, well..." He put away the map, and they trudged on.

Melmoth wasn't back to his usual health, getting tired quickly with the long day's hike. But he resented Lee's attempt to carry him, snarling and showing bared fangs at the boy.

"Leave him be," Dave said.

"He'll slow us down."

"Look at those mountains ahead, Lee. May not be a way through them. Not for us. Not for Sheever. Another hour or so won't make that much difference."

Zera sighed. "It'll be dark before we get to that town, Hope Springs, down there. I'd like a roof over my head in this cold weather."

"How cold you think it is, Dad?"

Dave spit. "Listen. Didn't ring on the ground. When it turns to ice in the air, then it's getting down."

Lee grinned. "I thought it got double-cold when your piss froze in your dick."

Dave nodded solemnly. "It's true, boy. It can snap off right in your hand there."

"Sure, Dad, sure."

HOPE SPRINGS had been built during the middle 2020s on the site of a small silver-mining settlement dating back a hundred and sixty years. Like Vail and some of the Colorado skiing resorts of the late 1900s, it had sprung from nothing, with rows of expensive condos available only to the superrich.

When the asteroid Adastreia, the inescapable, hit the Earth, the township was mainly deserted, with deep snow blocking most of the roads and filling in the runs.

It was so far out into the wilderness that it hadn't suffered as much as places that were nearer and more accessible to megacenters of population.

DUSK CAME SOFTLY across the land, heralded by a light mist that crept off the tops of the surrounding peaks. The temperature fell even lower. Dave grinned as he noticed Lee experimenting, spitting against a flat boulder at the side of the trail, hearing the clinking sound, like a fragment of glass, as the saliva turned to ice in the air.

From the winding track, marked with wheel ruts and the prints of hooves, they could look down into what remained of the township of Hope Springs.

"Lights," Zera said. "Quite a lot of them."

Dave took the Nikon lightweight glasses from around his neck and brought them to his eyes. But the evening was too far advanced to make out much except the dark blocks of the buildings clustered around an open square. At least twenty of them were showing lights, mainly the golden glow that he recognized as coming from oil lamps.

"We go in?"

"No. Can't tell if Sheever's there. He knows you. Could have made us back at the volcano if he had glasses on us. Best go in careful and easy. Find an empty place in the darkness on the edge of town."

"Anywhere out of the cold. Melmoth's shivering like he's got flu."

The young woman stooped and patted the pit bull, getting an appreciative whine from him.

BILLY KOTZWINKLE'S Krystal Emporium was the name on the sign above the log cabin. The door stood open, revealing an interior ravaged by looters. There was no sign of what the store had once sold, except for some torn and raggedy posters advertising prisms and magical pyramids. The floor was covered in faded brown carpet tiles, and a broken chair leaned in a corner. Behind what had once been the store, there was a small parlor, kitchen and bathroom.

All empty.

"Windows are sound," said Lee, casting his experienced eye around the building.

"Good hearth there, and we can scavenge for some wood. Have a fire in no time. There are still shutters on the windows, so nobody'll see us."

"Keying wonderful," Zera said.

An hour or so later there was still ice hanging in the corners of the ceiling. But within six feet of the fire, it was superbly warm.

Melmoth was deeply asleep, stretched out on the floor, belly exposed to the glowing heat. As a reward for his hard walking, Dave allowed the brindled animal to savor a whole tin of stew for himself.

They opened three more of their precious cans of meat, placing them in the bright embers at the front of the hearth, watching them slowly begin to steam and bubble. The scent of food filled the cabin, making them salivate.

"I'm goin' to eat mine now," Lee said eagerly, reaching for the can with gloved fingers.

"Don't. Wait until it really warms right through," warned his father. "Better in every way."

"Oh, Dad," he moaned, looking suddenly like a downcast child. Dave's heart softened at the flashback to when Lee had been a little boy, wanting to stay up to watch the final two quarters of Superbowl and being denied.

"All right . . . Have it when you like," Dave said, conscious of how his son had been robbed of a precious part of his adolescence by the disaster.

HE AND ZERA made love during the night.

It had been some time, and Dave reached his own urgent climax quickly. But the young woman took longer, seeming to balance forever on the edge of her own desperate precipice, pulling him in closer, heels locking in the small of the back, hips driving against him. It roused him to a second, rapid erection, helping to satisfy her. But now she came before he did, and Dave was left to battle on alone for a second time.

"For someone who used to be an accountant, you're sometimes useless at balancing the books, lover," she whispered, then softened the gibe with a gentle kiss on the lips.

"Get it right tomorrow," he replied. "But I was never very good at double entries."

THERE WAS some dried meat in Dave's pack, and he sliced it up into three large portions, with a smaller helping for Melmoth.

"Chew it thoroughly," he cautioned.

Outside there was the dim glow of the false dawn, full light still three-quarters of an hour away. A fall of snow during the night had covered the bare, hard earth with a frail layer of white. It was way below freezing in the derelict store, the fire having died away during the hours of darkness.

The dried meat was tough and gristly, and Dave found it seemed to be forming itself into a gigantic and totally indigestible lump. Struggling to breathe, he forced his jaws together.

"Aaargh!"

"What's wrong, Dad?"

"Groke 'uckin' 'ooth!"

"Broke your fucking tooth, Dave?" asked Zera.

He nodded, coughing out the lump of chewed meat into his palm and investigating it with his fingers. He held up something white. "'Ooth," he mumbled, poking at it some more and finding something else. A jagged piece of splintered bone.

"Maybe there'll be a dentist in Hope Springs," Lee said. "Don't forget how you said it was real sissy to make a fuss about a bit of toothache, Dad."

"'Uck off!" said Dave.

ZERA WENT IN FIRST, with Melmoth on a leash, to recon the township.

Dave and Lee checked through their collection of armaments. After some discussion, it had been agreed that the young woman would only carry the Ruger, concealed inside her parka, tucked into the leather belt.

The cold was so intense that Dave was worried about the bowstrings. With a bright, clear light lying across the valley, it would be potentially suicidal to try to get a fire going to warm them; any smoke would be visible for miles. He had a small container of grease in his pack, and he and Lee oiled the bows and fieldstripped the firearms. They checked the ammunition and finally honed their knives to a singing, razored sharpness.

Lee hefted Zera's Smith & Wesson 3000 12-gauge, clicking the folding stock into place. "Wouldn't mind this beauty," he said.

The pain from the broken tooth had abated, and Dave was able to talk more or less normally.

"If we have to move fast, then we gotta move light. Might have to ditch some we got."

"Come on, Dad."

"What you mean, 'Come on'?"

"It is Christmas, Dad."

"When?"

"Tomorrow."

"So what?"

7

Zera brought mixed news for them.

It was just after nine-thirty when they heard Melmoth barking. Lee went to cover the back of the Kotzwinkle store while his father watched out the front. But it was only the young woman, picking her way across the uneven ground toward them.

"Strange place," she said, clapping her hands together to warm them. The door was closed, shutting out the chill wind, giving the illusion that the cabin was just a little less cold.

"Strange?"

She took Melmoth off his lead, allowing the pit bull to go to flatten himself in front of the cold ashes of last night's fire.

"Yeah. Doesn't seem to have any real organization. Just a lot of people, doing the best they can."

"Sheever?" asked Dave.

"Yes."

Lee helped the young woman off with her parka, laying it across the broken chair. "Still there?"

"No. But he was in Hope Springs up to a couple of days ago. Been staying here for well over a week. From the people I spoke to, it looks like he's been losing men and animals. Most of them said he had about eight or nine with him.''

Reading Dave's question before he could even frame it, she added, "Yes, lover. The girls are *still* with them, and one woman said they looked in good shape. I didn't press her on it.''

"Sheever cause trouble?''

Zera shook her head. "Seems not much. Main problem that Hope Springs has is bunches of crazies passing through from the east. So far the citizens have held their lines. There's a couple of bodies dangling from a gallows as you walk down the main street. This woman, a widow named Ellen Williams, runs a kind of eatery, told me all this.''

"How about if we go in?''

"Why not?''

"Didn't see a dentist, did you?" Dave questioned, probing inside his mouth with an index finger, wincing at what he felt. "Snapped off jagged by the gum. Could fester and get an abscess. Might be someone in town.''

"Didn't see one. But there's plenty of buildings nearer that we could move into. The people just rip down empty houses and stores and apartment blocks of condos. Ellen Williams said that the expensive condos burn just as well as the cheap outhouses.''

"Can we go in, Dad?''

"Why not?''

IN SOME WAYS Hope Springs was the closest that Dave had seen to a normal town from before the long chill began. To a superficial observer, a lot of the streets appeared untouched by looters, with windows unbroken, facades undamaged.

But once they looked a little more closely, they saw the dust and the dirt, the neglect in the cracking paint and the withered gardens.

The first people they encountered, all wrapped in furs and warm clothing, looked at them suspiciously, hands creeping for hidden weapons. But the trio, with Melmoth trotting obediently at their heels, made a point of wishing everyone a bright "good morning" with a smile.

"The Williams woman lives down there," Zera said, pointing left at a crossroads.

"Could we stay with her?" Lee asked.

"Let's look around first," Dave replied.

"Hey, Dad!" Lee pointed with a gloved finger.

"What?"

"There."

"Come on, Lee," Zera sighed. "I'm not staying in a place like that."

Dave grinned. "Sounds the perfect place to spend Christmas Eve."

The sign was in flowing neon, ornate with curlicues and serifs. In the old days it would probably have flashed scarlet, off and on, catching the eye: Santa Claws' Adult Motel.

Underneath was a cracked plastic notice, listing some of the pleasures that the establishment had once offered.

Lee read them out. " 'Water beds in most rooms. Bookable by the hour. King- and queen-size. Adult movies and vids, rated Sextuple Sexy X. Hostesses available on request. Boox and mags for rent or purchase. Santa's Sex is Safest Sex.' "

"Hope Springs's finest porno palace," Zera snorted cynically.

"Might be a good place for a night," said Dave. "Let's go take a look."

There was another, smaller notice just by the front door to the two-story motel. It said, simply, Every Night Is Christmas Night At Santa Claws'.

Dave started around back down the street. A young boy was playing near the crossroads, and he stopped to peer at the three strangers. Beyond him there was the crude cross-tie of the gallows that Zera had mentioned. Two unidentifiable corpses dangled dryly in the cold easterly.

Lee followed his father's eyes. "Looks like hope's sprung for them," he said.

Not surprisingly the contents of the porno palace had been stripped months earlier. Anything that could be burned or eaten had gone, and most of the

rest was wrecked. But a tour of Santa's premises revealed some surprises.

Lee tied Melmoth up to the ornate iron balustrade
inside the front hallway.

At the end of the dark corridor, among the shadows, was a strange figure inside a cracked Plexiglas
case. There was a large red push-button on its front,
and the teenager pressed it.

The battery wasn't quite flat.

A scarlet bulb flared into life, illuminating the top
half of a life-size figure of an obscene-looking Father Christmas. The paint had been crudely applied
in the first place, and the passage of time had done
nothing to render it more delicate. The eyes were
staring orbs of aquamarine madness, the cheeks
veined in purple and maroon, like a meths drinker
under a midnight bridge. The hands ended in ver-
milion talons that waved and beckoned, as though
inviting the onlookers to participate in some hideous and blasphemous ritual.

The red robe was tatty, fringed with the ragged
remnants of white fur that had been devoured by
voracious insects. The whole dreadful entity rocked
unsteadily, as if it were in the grip of some drug-
induced madness, making the case vibrate and creak.
For an awesome moment Lee thought the whole
thing was about to break loose and lurch over the
patched lino toward him.

Then they heard the voice!

A slurred, fractured bass that bubbled through the speakers as though it had come through an infinite depth of molten phlegm.

"Ho, ho, ho ... Do I have a surprise for you, boys and girls.... Ho, ho, ho ... surprise ... boys ... surprise ... prise ... ho ... ho ... ho."

"Jesus," said Dave, standing behind his son. "I don't know what that does to the enemy, but it sure as hell terrifies me." Then he shrugged, and they resumed their inspection of the premises.

Every one of the vaunted water beds had been slashed to ribbons of rotting plastic and rubber, but they found a closet on the second floor that held a pile of blankets and bedding.

"Be cosy for once," Zera said, winking at Dave.

"Not with this tooth giving me rainbow pain every time cold air gets on it."

"Wasn't thinking of cold air, lover," she whispered as Lee left them to carry on his exploration.

The boy found a pile of torn magazines under a stained mattress and hefted them down to the front room, where an old fireplace waited for a fire.

"Could burn some of these, Dad," he said, chucking them on the floor.

"What are they?"

To Dave's embarrassment, his son blushed, the color spreading over the high, thin cheekbones. "Just some porno stuff, I guess."

"Let's look, sonny," smirked the young woman, bending over the ragged heap. "Probably some critical pix for jerk-off time."

Lee threw her the finger and went out. They stood in silence and heard his boots running up the bare staircase.

"Sorry, Dave," she said quietly. "I'll apologize to Lee in a while."

He nodded. "That's good."

She picked up a handful of the magazines, then whistled through her teeth at the illustrations.

"Look at this one. *Bicycle Seat Monthly!* Who gets off on bicycle seats?"

"I might. How about *Rubber Boots for Macho Males?* Turn you on?"

Zera looked at the front cover and giggled. "No. Sorry, lover, but no."

"Well, there's a story in this one called 'More Is Better.' Could be a goody. Or how about—"

She interrupted him. "Tell you what, David Alexander Rand."

"What?"

"Why don't we do like Lee suggested? And start a fire with the whole stupid pile of them?"

By early afternoon they'd done what they could to create warm nests of bedding for themselves. A fire was laid in the hearth, fed by the porno magazines.

Dave suggested that they might go and walk around the town. "And we could maybe find someone to do something about my tooth."

"Melmoth's tired. Why not leave him? Tie his lead to be safe and shut all the doors."

"Good idea, son."

"Just handguns?"

Dave opened his mouth to agree, but the door was open and an icy breeze brushed against the exposed nerves in the broken tooth, making him yelp.

"Was that a yes or a no, Dad?"

"'Ucking ess!"

THE BODIES HANGING from the crosspiece gallows looked as though they'd only been there a few days. Birds had taken the eyes and most of the face, leaving only strips of dried skin, peeled from the angle of the yellowed jaws. Finger bones clicked softly, like a distant rattler. Placards were strung around each neck, still legible.

Took What Wasn't Theirs To Take, they read.

Dave paused, looking at the corpses. "Long as there's still executions, you can be sure there's also some relics of society left."

"Dad!"

"What is it, Lee?"

For some reason there seemed to be a slightly malicious smile on the boy's face. He was pointing to a sign down a side street.

"What you wanted, Dad," he said.

The afternoon sun reflected brightly off the sign, carved and gilded in the shape of a huge human molar. Beneath it was the name. Rick Von Greede... Orthodontic Specialist.

"Yeah," said Dave. "Just what I wanted."

It was strange how the pain from his damaged tooth seemed to have suddenly disappeared.

8

Dave insisted that Zera and his son go off to explore Hope Springs, leaving him to face Rick Von Greede on his own. His excuse was that there was no point in all of them waiting around.

The truth was that David Rand had a long-standing and very deep-rooted terror of dentists, dating back to his youth when his mother had taken him to have a couple of his first teeth removed. He could still recall the building where the dentist lived.

A white frame house, with dark green shutters over the upstairs windows. The front door had rectangles of stained glass in it with twining flowers and mysterious vines in blue and gold. His mother had pulled on the brass bell, sending echoes through the building. Dave remembered pressing his nose against the glass and peering down an interminably long corridor. His friends had warned him about the horrors of going to the dentist, and he felt as though he were in imminent danger of filling his Fruit-of-the-Loom shorts.

There had been a shape, huge and white, wobbling toward him, the various hues of the glass making it change color with every step. It was vast, filling the doorway, with great goggling eyes.

By the time the overweight, bespectacled nurse had opened the door to let them in, Dave had been close to fainting.

Then there'd been the gas and the awful deadening lightness inside the skull. Floating and sinking, then jerking awake and gobbing clots of blood into the silver bowl.

Dave watched Lee and Zera until they'd turned the corner, then he summoned up all of his courage and turned the handle on the front door.

He was in a narrow, dusty hall, cold enough for his breath to gather around his face like a damp cloth. A scrawled arrow on the wall, labeled Dentist, pointed upward, and he followed it. There was no sense of life anywhere in the building, and he began to feel a mixture of hope and anxiety.

On the first landing he paused and looked around. There was a temptation to draw the Linebaugh, but he resisted it.

"Anyone here?" he called, his voice rising and falling about him.

The echoes spread out into stillness.

There was another arrow, this time directing him along a high-sided passageway that ran to the rear of the building. The doors on either side stood open, showing empty offices, dusty desks and rifled filing cabinets. The last door was ajar and bore a name in gold letters on the opaque glass.

Rick Von Greede . . . Orthodontist.

Dave's keen hearing caught the faint sound of rustling movement, and he drew the massive pistol, thumbing back on the hammer. He used the barrel to ease the door farther open.

"Hello?" he said.

"No answer came the stern reply," said a squeaky voice. "Shall we go? Yes, let's go. They do not move. Curtain."

Dave remained where he was, in the corridor. "You the dentist?" he asked.

"Is a raven a writing desk, or is that only when the wind is nor-nor-east? How when is up and where have all the flowers gone?"

Dave felt his patience slipping fast through his fingers, and he tightened the grip on the Linebaugh. "One more time, then I start getting seriously pissed at you. Are you the dentist?"

There was a giggle, like a nervous schoolboy. "A person of intemperate spirits. Wanting a dentist. Oh, my goodness, yes. Do come in, sir. Come in."

The handgun pushed the door the rest of the way open to reveal a waiting room with a dozen canvas-backed chairs lined up around the walls. A central table, one leg propped up by a brick, held a pile of dog-eared magazines. A second door stood ajar.

The room was empty.

"Come right on through. No waiting in this dental practice."

Dave walked on through, finding himself in the familiar dental consulting room. There was the reclining chair, maroon leather, with a light poised over it and a white side tray covered in a jumble of glittering steel instruments.

Dave quickly looked away to size up the man who reclined in a narrow chair, his feet propped up on a stool. He was in his fifties, with a shock of white hair. He had large glasses with frames the color of Kansas wheat and a suit that had clearly gone too long since its last visit to a cleaner. He was holding a dog-eared paperback in his bony fingers, the cover still bright with its bold design of psychedelic colors.

"Dr. Von Greede?" Dave asked, holstering the Linebaugh.

"What a superb handgun, mister...?"

"Rand. Dave Rand."

"Mr. Rand. Looks like it could blow a hole through a lawman's conscience. Care to trade for it? Do you a full set of porcelain crowns, top and bottom, and throw in any incidental root canal work, as well."

He uncoiled from the chair, and now Dave saw that his long chin showed a silvery film of stubble.

"No. Thanks, but no. Just got a broken tooth, and I wondered if . . . ?"

"If my skilled hands and wealth of medical skill could possibly ameliorate your bitter suffering?"

Despite his discomfort, Dave grinned. "Something like that."

"Sit ye down, sit ye down." He pulled on a whitish apron and gestured at the chair. "Sorry, but none of the hydraulics work. Bit of a power problem in Hope Springs."

"I've noticed that in other towns," Dave replied, struggling to control his nervousness and folding his hands to try to keep them still.

"You have all the calm of a skittish colt, Mr. Rand. Should I seek to gentle you by stroking your head, or should I offer you a lump of sugar? Ah, a small problem. No sugar. Must go and trade with the Widow Williams. Still has the best store of food in town."

"How do I pay you for this tooth?" Dave asked, sitting up as the dentist began to lean forward with mirror and probe in hand.

"Food?"

"We got some cans of stew."

Von Greede straightened and put his head on one side consideringly. "Stew?"

"Beef. With beans."

"Wouldn't have any chicken, Thai-style, would you? With a smattering of coconut rice?"

"No."

The dentist sighed. "Story of my life. Haven't had a patient yet who was able to offer me that. Best have a look inside your buccal orifice, and then we can negotiate a deal based on the stew index."

Dave leaned back again, looking at the ceiling, which showed bizarre patterns of damp mildew, like surreal archipelagoes and isthmuses. His mouth opened, and he felt the dentist's fingers probing. There was the chink of chromed steel on enamel.

"Oooow!"

"Sorry." The dentist paused. "Why do I bother saying that? I'm not really the least bit sorry, Mr. Rand. You have a badly broken molar, lower left. And you could do with some fillings and possibly..."

"'Ust 'ooth."

"How's that?" Von Greede asked, taking his probe away.

"Just the tooth. Maybe take it out so I don't have any more problems with it. Not many dentists practicing now."

"Sad but true. Very well. I'll extract it, but it might be a little...how shall I put it?"

"Painful?"

"Very."

"If there's no power, how are you going to drill or fill or whatever?"

"No drill. No fill. Just a stout pair of pliers and my right hand. Looks like a job for knee-in-the-chest man."

Dave closed his eyes. He was glad that he'd suggested Zera and Lee leave him alone while Rick Von Greede did the business on his damaged tooth.

The skinny dentist gave him three injections to try to dull the pain, but it didn't stop the sickening sounds and the taste of blood. There was so little tooth remaining above the the gum that Von Greede had to slice through with a scalpel to open it enough to get a grip with the forceps.

Even then it was a struggle.

After another chunk had splintered off, the dentist stood back for a breather. "Mind if I ask you what you used to do, Dave?"

"Accountant."

"Explains a lot. Never had a patient so reluctant to part with a bit of himself."

Dave was surprised that much of the initial pressure was inward, pushing, and it only switched to shaking and pulling at the end of the operation. There was a sound as though a tenement block were being demolished in his mouth, and then a great feeling of release. A rush of warm, salty blood, and it was done.

"There," said Von Greede, triumphantly flourishing the shattered fragments in his crimsoned fingers. "Want to keep it for the tooth fairy, Dave?"

"No thanks, Rick."

"I think we can just about get by without imposing needle and thread on you. Little pain for a day or so, but I'll give you something for that. Now, rinse it out, and we can talk about cans of stew."

While Dave recovered, the two men talked quietly. The dentist was interested in the quest and confirmed that Sheever's stay in town had been made necessary by falling numbers among his gang.

"Sickness and brutality, mostly. But I saw your daughters, and they seemed in fine shape. Amazing, considering everything that . . ."

Dave nodded, holding the side of his face gingerly. "Not long before I catch up and get 'em free. Jesus, you sure you didn't take out the jawbone and left the tooth?"

"It'll be tender. Eat slop for today."

"How about stew?"

Rick grinned. "Truth is . . . Hope Springs must have had more well-stocked closets than any comparable town in the whole country. And fewer people. That's why the crazies come, having heard of days of wine and roses and honey. But folks here are cautious and well organized."

"Saw the gallows."

"Been lots of that strange fruit turning in the wind and sun, Dave. And there will be plenty more."

"That why Sheever didn't take over here like he has in other places?"

"Guess so. I saw him a few times, and he didn't seem a happy man. Like someone had ripped away his favorite security blanket."

Dave rubbed his jaw again, feeling the swelling, but the blood wasn't flowing so quickly. "But what happens to Hope Springs in a couple of years?"

"When the supplies are gone?"

"Yeah. Then what?"

The dentist stood up and went to a small desk. He unlocked a side drawer and reached far inside it. Dave heard a faint click as though a hidden lock had been sprung. Von Greede straightened, holding a brown bottle.

"My exit passes to a far, far better rest that I go to, than I have ever known."

"Sydney Carton," Dave said, pleased with himself for identifying the quotation. He must have been in about the fifth grade when he'd read *Tale of Two Cities.*

The dentist snapped his fingers and stooped to replace the bottle of tablets. "Excellent, Dave. He's remembered as the hero, but Dickens said that Carton would never have made a good lion but he made a remarkably fine jackal."

"Better be going. You're sure about the stew?"

"Absolutely, my dear fellow. And remember my suggestion to look up the merry widow."

"Ellen Williams?"

"Correct."

"Might do that. Santa Claws' porno palace has a stout roof and walls, but the decor leaves a lot to be desired."

"Know what you mean. I did some nice bridge-work for Millie Whitehouse. Oh, Santa Claws to you. Sweetest old lady you'd meet in a country mile. Died a few months ago in her eightieth year. Sleeps with the angels. Sure she's in Abraham's bosom."

"Gotta go. Thanks for helping me out."

He shook hands with Rick Von Greede, surprised at the power of the thin man's grip.

"Take care. And good luck with the quest for your daughters."

Dave nodded and left the room, past the table of dead magazines in the waiting area and down the dusty stairs into the cold street.

A young girl was sitting on the boardwalk opposite him, playing with a plastic soldier doll. She looked up at him, wary eyed, gathering herself ready to run.

"Hi, there," Dave said.

"Your mouth's bleeding, mister," she replied.

He touched his finger to the corner of his lips and brought it away smeared with bright blood.

"Thanks for telling me."

"You're welcome." She picked up her doll and scampered away down a side alley.

Dave watched her go and then resumed walking down into the center of the town to rejoin Lee and Zera.

9

"Your boy's been splitting wood for me. Earned enough for our flat-rate meal."

Ellen Williams was a few pounds the wrong side of plump. Her cerise tracksuit was very tight around the hips, its high collar emphasizing the extra layer of chins. She was tall, close to six feet, with broad shoulders. Hearing strangers, she had come out from the steamy kitchen, her cheerful face dappled with sweat.

Her daughter, Leeanne, was a sulky teenager, skinny where her mother was fat. She served tables in the bustling town eatery.

"What's the flat-rate meal?"

Ellen Williams pointed to the wall, where a board carried a chalked menu. "That's it, Mr. Rand. What you see is what there is." She rested a fleshy hand on his shoulder, letting it remain there for several seconds. Dave noticed that Zera had seen the gesture.

"Just had a tooth pulled. Best go easy for today."

"Rick do you a good job?" She didn't wait for him to reply. "Course he did. Sweet bastard. Anyways, take your time and tell my little girl here what you want." She smiled at Lee. "How old are you, son?"

"Sixteen."

"Leeanne's seventeen. Hey, Lee and Leeanne. Goes together real nice."

Someone called to her from the kitchen, and she turned on her heel and swung away, leaving her daughter standing by them, notebook and pen in her hand.

"You decided yet?" she said.

"I'll have the potato soup," Dave said. "And the chocolate-fudge cake."

"Sure." She turned to Zera. "You?"

"No soup. Ham and grits with black-eyed peas. Fudge cake."

Leeanne wrote it down slowly, biting at her lower lip. When she came to Lee, the tight, sullen mouth broadened into a dazzling smile. "How about you, Lee? The venison pie's real good. And the pecan ice cream."

Dave watched his son's face, seeing his reaction to the girl. Leeanne was undeniably pretty, in a tight pair of stone-washed jeans and a frilly white blouse, low and close fitted. Her blond hair was flounced out around her face. She teetered in a pair of dark green Western boots with high heels.

"I'd like the venison pie and then I'll try the pecan ice cream. Please."

"You're welcome, Lee. Sure you wouldn't like some soup to begin?"

"No, thanks."

"Coffee?"

"Yes, please."

"Sure thing."

As she moved away from their table, Zera called after her. "Miss?"

"What?" she threw over her shoulder.

"I'd like some coffee, too. Dave?"

"Why not?"

"That'll be three coffees, then."

Leeanne muttered something and vanished into the kitchen through the double swinging doors.

"Service with a smile," Zera said.

Nobody else spoke much to them in the place except for the odd question about where they'd come from and where they were going. Had they seen any crazies on the trail? Good hunting to the east of Hope Springs? There was a preoccupation with horses. It seemed that there'd been a spate of rustling from local homes and farms, but nobody had been able to catch any of the thieves.

"We catch 'em and we hang 'em," said a lean old man with a bristling white mustache.

"Why not?" Dave said.

The food had been a little better than adequate, though the potato soup had been lumpy and the coffee so weak that you could have read a newspaper through it.

Ellen kept slipping out from her domain, checking on the food and constantly asking Dave if he wanted more. How was his tooth? Did he need more water or coffee?

Lee was pestered by Leeanne. His plate was piled to overflowing with food, gravy spilling on the table, mashed potato like a snowy mountain.

While they sat over their coffee, Zera looked at the two men. "I have to say that playing wallflower to that fat widow and her simpering daughter is not my idea of a fucking fun meal."

Dave laid a hand on her wrist, gripping it when she tried to pull away. "Listen. I feel like shit with this jaw. Tomorrow's Christmas Day, and it would be real good to spend it somewhere other than the adult motel up the street."

"Stay with *them,* Dad?"

"They take in boarders."

Zera finally tugged her hand away from him. "You'll both finish up either raped or married!"

Dave shook his head. "Come on."

"Or both!"

IT WAS the sort of house where the sun needed to knock and ask permission to enter in the mornings—and would probably be told to wipe its feet first.

The only other guest was an elderly woman named Caitlin Probert, a schoolteacher from Iowa who'd been passing through Hope Springs when Adastreia impacted. Her speciality had been domestic science, and the Widow Williams allowed her to cook in the eatery in return for bed and board.

Dave, Lee and Zera returned briefly to the porno hotel to retrieve Melmoth and the remainder of their weapons and possessions. After coming back in the afternoon to the center of the town, they headed east a hundred yards along Jefferson to the Victorian house.

Zera's initial reluctance to stop a night with the widow and her eager daughter was overcome by the comfort of their house.

There was a bedroom for each of them, brushed clean and scented with lavender. Sprigged muslin dominated the decorations, and each bed was brass framed and covered with a flowered comforter. A gas generator thudded away at the back of the house, providing both heat and light.

Dave had developed a grinding headache from his visit to the dentist and elected to go to his room early, just after nine.

There was a row of dog-eared paperbacks on the shelf below the window, and he'd noticed a collection of the works of Allen Ginsberg, one of his favorite poets from the previous century.

He undressed and wriggled down into the cool, clean sheets. But he'd barely begun to read "Kaddish" when there was a soft rapping on the door.

"Shit," he said under his breath.

"David?" The voice insinuated itself through the large keyhole. "Are you asleep?"

He considered whether he could get away with saying yes. Or perhaps he could ignore the voice. It might go away if he did.

But the knocking was repeated, louder this time and followed by the honeyed voice. "David, are you there? I have a passkey if you're not well."

"Oh, no, here it comes," he mumbled to himself through gritted teeth. "I'm coming, Ellen."

She was wearing a lilac pantsuit, her hair permed into rigid waves, so sharp he feared he might cut himself if he brushed against them. There was a sweeping aura of perfume about her that literally took his breath away.

"I just wondered if you wanted anything." She didn't quite say *Anything,* but very nearly.

"No. I'm fine. Just feel tired." He made a token move toward shutting the bedroom door, sensing that it would fail.

Ellen sighed and stepped into the room, helping him to close the door behind her. "I can't bear to think of you being alone on the night before Christmas." She giggled. "Not even a mouse moving, Dave."

He was glad he'd kept on his shirt and shorts. It gave him a fragile reserve of security.

"I'm really tired. And my jaw hurts like hell. You don't . . ." Then he couldn't think how to finish the sentence.

"I don't what?" she said, moving so close her hip brushed against his.

"I think I should get to bed early."

"So do I."

"I mean so I can be fresh for tomorrow."

"I'm feeling fresh tonight, Dave. Oh, there's so much I want to talk to you about."

He backed away, until the edge of the bed pressed against the back of his knees. "What you want to say?"

"You must have noticed that my eatery is a little gold mine, Dave."

"Sure."

"And you know we're having more and more trouble with crazies and gangs like that bastard Sheever coming through Hope Springs."

"I know."

"And that I'm a widow. And my little girl and your little boy have hit it off together real nice."

That wasn't quite how Dave had seen it, but he didn't interrupt her.

"What we need, Dave—" She had moved even closer, trapping him so that he couldn't even escape back onto the bed. "We need a couple of dependable men to look after us, Leeanne and me. Real men. Look after us both and be a husband for me and a father for Leeanne, and a son for me and a friend...a good, good friend for Leeanne. Won't you help us out, Dave?"

The knock on the door made them both start. Ellen jumped toward Dave, and he had nowhere to go but flat on his back on top of the bed, drawing the widow with him.

The door was flung open, letting in a draft of cold air from the corridor.

Dave, muffled under scented flesh, couldn't turn his head to see who it was. But he recognized the voice.

"Getting your Christmas present a few hours early, lover?"

It took a few uncomfortable, flustered minutes, with apologies all around, but everyone was conscious that nobody really meant what they were saying.

Eventually Ellen Williams backed out, her face pink, saying she hoped that he...they...slept well and wishing them a Merry Christmas.

Almost immediately the door opened again, and in walked Lee, grinning broadly. "Old lady looks like she found a used condom in her malted milk. What happened, Dad?"

"Nothing happened." He looked at Zera. "I tell you *nothing* happened at all."

"Sure, Dad, sure. Keep your teeth in."

"Go walk Melmoth, Lee. Do something useful."

"Fine. G'night."

"Think I'll be going to bed also," Zera said. "I suspect the living room downstairs might be a little on the cold side right now. Know what I mean?"

She kissed him gently on the cheek and went out of the room.

RICK HAD GIVEN Dave a couple of painkillers, and he took them in a glass of water. His jaw was throbbing and his head ached, but he eventually slipped into an uneasy sleep.

Later in the night he found himself in a hideous dream. His right knee had somehow been honeycombed by fat black worms, a couple of inches long. When he tried to grab at them, they simply slithered between his finger and thumb and vanished down the red-rimmed maze of tunnels in his flesh.

He woke trembling and sweating to find that the first pale light of the new Christmas Day was already peeping through the drapes.

10

"Happy Christmas, Roxanne," Ellie said, squeezing her little sister's hand beneath the warmth of the sleeping bag.

"And to you, Ellie."

The two girls lay in the dawn light beneath the frozen, snow-topped trees, hugging each other. The remains of Sheever's gang slept all around them, and the horses snickered softly by the ice-glazed stream.

For several minutes neither of them spoke, and both pretended not to notice that the other was crying.

CAITLIN PROBERT provided a fine breakfast spread, under express orders from the widow to give the visitors the very best.

When Dave came down to join Zera and Lee, the table was groaning with good things laid out on decent china with Ellen Williams's silver wedding cutlery gleaming at every place.

The widow herself shone from the head of the table, with her blank-faced daughter at her side.

"Welcome, welcome, David. And a very merry Christmas to you and your son and to your friend."

The warmth of the greeting dropped several degrees when she reached Zera.

"Thank you, and the same to you."

He went first to his son. Lee stood up awkwardly, hugging his father to him and kissing him on the side of his stubbled cheek. "Happy Christmas, Dad," he mumbled.

"And to you. With my love and thanks and...I'm very proud of you, son. Sorry I haven't been able to get you a present this year. Maybe next year."

"Sure, Dad. I couldn't find anything in the stores for you, either."

Zera had washed her hair, and it was still slightly damp. Her blue eyes sparkled against the blond mane as she stood and kissed him demurely on the cheek.

"Cool Yule, lover," she said.

"And you. Wish I could have got you a little something. Good to have you along with us."

She put her mouth against his ear, speaking so quietly that he could hardly hear her. "Maybe your little something and my little something can get together later?"

"Maybe, Zera, maybe."

"Pardon me for interrupting, but there's some good eating going to waste here. We got clam chowder and chicken-fried steak and a stack of buckwheat cakes. Three kinds of syrup. Offer them to Lee, there's a good girl, Leeanne."

"Cinnamon and blueberry and honey. Which would you like, Lee?"

"I'll take the blueberry, thanks."

"You're welcome."

"Your daughter's eyes get any bigger, Mrs. Williams," Zera said tartly, "and they'll fall right out on her plate."

"Surely, dear. How 'bout you? Looks like you've already eaten more than your fill, but I figure you can find room for some more. There's ham and some trout and a mess of eggs and hash browns."

"Just a slice of toast and some black coffee, thank you."

The meal crawled past, everyone uncomfortable with Mrs. Williams's fawning attention to Dave and Leeanne's simpering friendliness toward Lee.

At last they were done, and Dave went out alone. Ellen Williams had promised them a fine Christmas supper at six. Turkey and all the trimmings. Since they were guests in her house, Dave didn't feel they could leave until the next morning.

But he used his time profitably, going around the town and hunting up horses. Finally he learned that there were some for sale at a spread about four miles to the west of Hope Springs.

He returned early in the afternoon and updated Lee and Zera. "Man I spoke to said to be sure and get a signed bill of sale. All the thieves around here have made everyone cautious."

"Then we go after Sheever tomorrow?" Lee's eyes danced at the prospect.

"Yes. Bid farewell to the ladies of the house first."

Zera's eyes gleamed wickedly. "Rather you than me, lover."

THE SUN HAD BROKEN through around noon but the temperature remained stubbornly in the minus twenties.

Lee and Zera took Melmoth for a long walk up into the bleak hills. At Dave's insistence that they take both handguns and a scattergun with them, Zera picked the Smith & Wesson 3000, while Lee suggested to his father that the Czech Skorpion machine pistol might not be a bad idea.

"If there's crazies out in the mountains, like everyone says there is."

"Sure. I'm going to rest up some. Didn't sleep enough, what with my jaw hurting. Take care, Lee."

He'd watched them out the front door, walking together along Jefferson and then vanishing at the crossing. His fingers rose to touch his cheek. The bleeding had stopped from the socket, but the gum was swollen and tender.

Dave headed back up to his room and ran into Caitlin Probert in the main-floor hallway.

He stopped and flashed her a friendly glance. "Supper going to be good?"

"I do hope so, Mr. Rand. But the gas generator is proving a little unreliable, which means the temperature of the oven doesn't hold true. But I shall do my best."

He smiled and climbed the stairs, closing the door of his room and stretching out on the brass bed. The air was chilled, and he tugged the comforter over him, closing his eyes.

Sleep came easily, and for once he dozed quietly, dreamlessly, sliding into a gentle darkness.

"Don't move or you get to be dead." The voice was low and determined.

His eyes twitched open, and he started to sit up but felt the double pricking of sharp knives digging into his throat just under the angle of the jaw. He kept still and looked around.

Ellen Williams sat on one side of the bed, leaning over him, the handle of the needle-pointed carving knife set against his neck. Leeanne matched her on the other side, with a narrow-bladed skinning knife. The girl was giggling under her breath.

"Doesn't he look surprised, Ma?" she whispered.

"I am surprised," he said, swallowing to clear the dryness from his throat.

"I've been talking to my little girl...about how you didn't want to stay with us. And we thought that it wasn't right."

"Go on. I'm listening."

Leeanne giggled louder, pushing the point of the knife so hard that Dave felt a tiny thread of warmth on his throat. "He says that he's listening to us, Ma!"

"It's life or death, Dave. We can't go on like this. We *need* a man. Two men, with your son."

"How about Zera?"

The woman smiled, and Dave felt his bowels lurch with fear. "Easy to put her out of the way. Won't be the first."

"And we stay here, Lee and me...and help you? That it?"

"That's it."

He realized then that the cheerful widow was a lot less than ninety cents on the dollar. Maybe less than fifty cents. But that didn't make the threat any less real, and in some ways it made it a whole lot worse.

"What if..." he started to say, then decided that asking her about how she'd enforce any agreement wasn't a good idea. There was some murky water that you just didn't dip your toes into.

"What if what?"

"What if you let Zera go?"

The eyes narrowed. "Could be. You think she'd just up and walk?"

"She doesn't care that much for me or for Lee. We're just traveling meal-tickets to her. When I tell her what we've agreed on, I think she'd go happily."

"Let her, Ma. I really hate all the blood from killing. Gets down my nails."

"Fine. You tell her, Dave. But if she makes trouble..." The tip of the steel pushed a little harder, making him gulp.

"Sure."

"So you agree?"

He nearly nodded but stopped himself in time and kept his head still. "Course I do. I can see now what a good life we can all have. And Leeanne'll be a real daughter to me."

"Yeah..." The next thing she said made him wish he'd not mentioned his daughters. "How about your girls?"

"They're lost. I'd more or less decided to give up the chase, anyway. I told Lee that only last night."

"You did?"

"Sure."

"Maybe he's lying, Ma," said Leeanne suspiciously. "Tricking us."

"That it, Dave?"

"No. I told you. If I tried to trick you, it'd be easy for you to kill me, wouldn't it?"

"How?"

"Wait until I'm asleep."

She nodded slowly, and a big smile spread over her cheeks. "Right. Then it's a deal. Got to find a way of sealing the bargain." The fingers of her left hand slipped under the covers and reached for him. His body jerked, but the two knives kept him still.

Ellen's hand pushed insistently inside his briefs, scrabbling for him. She found what she was after and slowly began to rub and squeeze.

Then her movements became faster.

Leeanne stared into his eyes. "He's loving it, Ma. Like a kitten having its fur rubbed."

Dave blinked. Despite the horror of his own situation, he felt himself responding to her skilled manipulation.

"Getting there, Dave. I think you best go out, Leeanne. I can handle this for a half hour or so."

The girl stood up, still holding her knife. She was grinning vacantly. "You sure can handle him, Ma."

In the cold room, Dave was conscious that both women had been drinking. The reek of vodka hung about them sickeningly.

Ellen's fingers moved faster, squeezing, bringing him perilously close to climax. Her eyes locked to his. "Don't spurt your roll yet, lover," she warned. "Once my little girl's left us, we'll find a better use for this."

Leanne was at the door, but she had turned to watch them. The Widow Williams had allowed the knife to move from his throat, but it was still only inches away.

"How about allowing me to get comfortable and share a kiss?" he said.

"Why not?"

She sat up, smiling at him, licking her lips. Dave swung his legs over the side of the bed and stood, pulling her to her feet. His erection was rock hard, thrusting between them.

Ellen held the carving knife down at her side and turned her face up to him, closing her eyes.

He gripped her by the shoulders with a massaging motion of his hands, then smashed his forehead down onto the bridge of her nose.

Bone crushed like a ripe apple in the fist of a strong man. Dave had instinctively closed his eyes at the impact, and he opened them to see the woman's face turn into a mask of flowing blood. The knife dropped to the floor, and Ellen Williams crumpled after it. As she fell, she groaned in pain and shock.

"You dirty fucker..." began her daughter, taking a half step toward Dave, raising her own blade to shoulder height and making a clumsy attempt to stab him.

Dave parried the blow easily, moving inside it. He punched her once in the stomach, twisting his fist on impact to give it a more devastating effort.

Leeanne gasped and doubled over, clutching at herself. A mixture of vodka and yellow bile frothed from her gaping lips, splattering on the carpet. Dave moved back and punched her once more on the side of the neck, knocking her unconscious.

As he turned, he saw that Ellen was struggling to her feet. She'd regained possession of the long-bladed knife and was stepping in his direction, raising the knife in the air. Crimson blood bubbled from her pulped nose, over her mouth, tumbling in a bright sheen over her chest. She mumbled something, but the injury and the blood muffled her words. She swung the knife in an arc, the pain fueling her rage.

Dave dodged past her and drew the Linebaugh from its holster. Holding three and a half pounds of metal by the walnut butt, he hefted it and brought it down on the woman's temple.

The sound of the blow was oddly muted, a soft impact that hardly jarred his wrist. But Ellen pitched down on her face, fingers scrabbling at the carpet. Her body jerked, legs flailing, rolling her onto her back. There was a sudden stillness, and she lay unmoving, eyes staring blindly at the ceiling.

"Oh, Christ!" said Dave. It hadn't gone the way he wanted. But he'd been out on the ragged edge of survivalism long enough to know that violence wasn't something that came in neat, measured doses.

Leeanne was deeply unconscious, lying on her side, knees huddled up under her.

Dave looked down at the girl, trying to decide what he should do.

Zera and Lee would be returning from their walk with Melmoth in a half hour or so. And then Caitlin Probert would be serving up the Christmas turkey with all the trimmings.

The room stank of vomit, sweat and the smell of the alcohol that both mother and daughter had been drinking.

It was that scent of vodka that offered Dave a solution to his problem.

He stepped carefully around the corpse of the Widow Williams and stood over her daughter.

Trying to breathe through his open mouth, he stopped by Leeanne and reached for her.

11

"More turkey, Mr. Rand?"

"Thank you, Caitlin."

"Brown meat or white?"

"Bit of each, please. It's really delicious. Just what a fowl should be. Crisp on the outside and tender and moist on the inside."

"Shame that Mrs. Williams and her daughter aren't here. I mean, it is Christmas, after all."

The cook sliced some meat and placed it on Dave's plate, then added a serving of sweet potatoes with some carrots and broad beans.

"I'll help myself to the stuffing and cranberry sauce."

"And the gravy, Mr. Rand," she urged. "I'm particularly proud of my gravy."

Both Zera and Lee were aware that something had gone seriously wrong, but Dave deliberately hadn't told them what it was. It was crucial that Caitlin Probert didn't suspect that murder had been done. So the more natural everyone was, the better their chances of getting away with it.

Dave hadn't wanted to sneak away from Hope Springs at dusk. It was better by far to make a fresh start at dawn.

Melmoth lay flat on his belly near Lee's chair, gnawing on the scraps of meat that the boy tossed down to him.

"Should I go knock on Mrs. Williams's door and see if she's feeling like coming down to join us?" asked Caitlin Probert. "I just feel she's going to be so unhappy about missing all this good cheer."

Dave shook his head. "No. Truth is—" He picked up his wineglass and emptied it, then mimed draining it again, making his hand tremble.

The cook sighed. "Oh, it's so sad the way that woman drinks liquor. And she takes her daughter down that same slippery path with her."

"Amen to that," Dave said piously. He lifted his knife and fork and tucked into the supper. A trickle of rich gravy seeped down his chin, and he wiped it away, finally licking his fingers.

It was a good meal and a fine ending to a troubled Christmas Day, though the day wasn't quite ended.

After Caitlin Probert had cleared away the dishes from the brandied pudding, Zera touched Dave on the arm. "Word before we all go to bed."

"Sure."

"Your room?"

"No."

"Why not?"

"Changed my room. Preferred one overlooking the street."

"My room?"

"Sure."

"Now?"

Dave straightened in his chair. "Lee? We're going to have a Christmas talk in Zera's room."

"Sure, Dad."

The cook came back in at that moment, carrying porcelain cups of coffee. She smiled at them warmly. "How nice. A family talk on Christmas night."

ZERA SHUT THE DOOR of her room and sat on the bed. Lee took an armchair, and Dave stood by the window, looking blankly out at the starry night. Melmoth lay contentedly on the floor by the empty hearth.

"Now, Dave, what the fuck is going on here? Where's the widow and her brat?"

"Dead."

Outside the window, farther down the street, they could all hear a drunk bellowing out the greetings of the season to anyone who was listening. In the room nobody spoke for several long seconds.

"Dead?" said Zera. "Both of them?"

"No. The Widow. Came at me with a knife. I didn't have any real choice."

"How about Leeanne, Dad? What did you do to her?"

"Laid her out. Tied and gagged her. Locked her in my old room."

"You do have a way with the ladies, lover," said Zera.

"When do we leave?"

"First light, like we usually do. Tell Caitlin we're heading back east. No, don't tell her. Leave a note. Then we're away."

"Tell her what happened. Say it was an accident and tell her that the girl's tied up in the locked room."

Dave shook his head. "No. Less said the better."

Zera insisted. "But she might die in . . ."

"First thing she'll do is look and check my room. She'll find them both there."

Zera got up from the bed and joined him by the window. He deliberately didn't face her, and she took his arm. "Dave."

"Don't, Zera."

"The daughter?"

"Just leave it," he said, eyes blank as a cruising shark, mouth set in a tight, metallic line. "I'll decide."

Lee also stood up, suddenly realizing what it was they were talking about. "Dad?"

"I'm not discussing this. I had two crazed bitches both holding knives at my jugular! What I did is what I did. And in the morning we're getting out of Hope Springs, and with luck we're away free. Talk won't change any of that."

"But the girl was . . ."

Dave took a half step toward his son, fist clenching, close as he'd ever been to slapping him across the mouth. "Enough, Lee."

"Su Sure, good night, Dad. Come on, Melmoth."

He closed the bedroom door very quietly behind him, leaving Dave alone with Zera.

She looked at him in silence. "Dave—" She held up her hand as he started to speak. "No. I just want to know if you're going to tell me about it or not."

"Not," he said.

"Fine." She nodded slowly. "You have to do what you think best, lover. And then you have to live with it." Turning away from him, she walked to the door and opened it, then paused and looked back at him over her shoulder. "Happy Christmas, Dave." Silently she closed the door.

During the night Dave cat-footed along the moonlit corridor and fumbled with the key to his old room. The house shifted and creaked in the darkness as he went to the closet. There he saw Leeanne's still form, with no sign of life fluttering in the cold wrist. She had choked on her own vomit. Relieved that he didn't have to make a decision, Dave returned to his own bed. In the house nobody stirred.

DAVE WOKE before the first chill warning of the false dawn and went down to put a scribbled note on the table in the kitchen. He returned upstairs again to wake the others and collect their gear.

Both of them were already awake when he tapped on their doors.

"See you out front in five minutes," he said.

He found Caitlin Probert in the shadowed hall, his note in her right hand. Her hair was tied back and covered with a fine net, and she wore a faded blue dressing gown. Dave noticed that her feet were bare.

"You're going east, Mr. Rand." It wasn't exactly a question and not quite a statement, yet it somehow contrived to imply that the woman didn't believe a word of it.

"Possibly."

Her left hand was in the pocket of her dressing gown. Her eyes steady on his face, she pulled out a bunch of labeled brass keys. "Duplicates, Mr. Rand."

He nodded. Above him he could hear Melmoth whining with excitement at going out once more. In the hall there was only the sonorous ticking of an oak-cased grandfather clock.

"I have been in what was your bedroom, Mr. Rand," she said.

"And?"

She sighed and put the keys back in her pocket. "It was bound to happen sooner or later, the way that she . . . But I would not speak ill of the dead."

For some reason Dave felt he wanted to try to explain to this quiet woman what had happened. "She and . . ." he began.

"Better I hear nothing. And until this afternoon, I shall also see nothing."

"And after that?"

Something that might have been the ghost of a smile flitted across her face. "I shall *not* say nothing, Mr. Rand. I shall rouse the township with what I've found. They might manage a half-hearted posse and chase you. Chase you east, of course. But that will not be for at least seven or eight hours."

"Thanks, Caitlin."

"No. The Widow Williams and her daughter were not much loved in town. Not if the truth were known. And the men would rather hunt a horse thief than three strangers, well armed, who have killed. . . . You take my meaning?"

"Yes."

"So, go. I'm returning to my bed now."

Dave couldn't think of anything to say to the woman other than "Thanks."

"And I hope you find your little girls."

THEY MADE GOOD TIME westward, mostly covering ground in silence. Dave chose not to mention the meeting with Caitlin Probert.

They reached the ranch in just over two hours' brisk walking. It was off a side trail on a steep highway into the mountains. There was a hand-painted notice on the main track, which Dave read aloud.

"We got horses and we trade. We have plenty of firepower and shoot troublemakers. So trade or keep moving."

"What happened to old-fashioned courtesy and service?" Zera remarked.

It was virtually the first thing she'd said all morning, and Dave took it to mean that things were returning to normal. Lee also saw it that way, and a three-way conversation resulted.

"What do we trade, Dad?"

"Guns."

"But we need them."

"Need horses more."

"We caught up with Sheever when we were on foot," said Zera. Reconsidering, she added, "Though I guess some of the best times we had some kind of help."

"Dry, cold weather like this, and he can just ride away from us," said Dave.

"We know we're still on the right trail. Once we lose them..." Lee allowed his words to drift away into the chill morning.

There was confirmation that they were still in reasonable contact with Sheever's group when they reached the Duvall spread.

It was more like a fortified prison than a traditional ranch, which was probably why it was still functioning. The trail narrowed between walls of rock until they reached a massive metal-and-wood gate that completely blocked off the canyon. A bell-pull hung on the right with another of Duvall's friendly notices: This Is For Business And You Better Be Serious.

Lee tugged on the handle, but they couldn't hear any sound.

They waited for what seemed an eternity, the only noise the wind blowing through the tops of the forest of pines on either side. Lee rang the bell twice more.

"We keep on waiting?" Zera asked. "I'm getting seriously cold here."

Dave looked around. If Caitlin Probert had been lying, then they might find a posse on their heels in the next half hour, and there was nowhere to run to up there.

"Ring it one more time, Lee."

"No need, friend." The voice came from a hatch that had silently opened at one side of the gate. Dave glanced to his left and saw a second slit opening up. What looked like the barrels of light machine guns poked through, covering them.

"Come to trade for three horses and maybe a pack animal. You got that?"

The voice that replied was flat and neutral, sounding as though it belonged to someone who was used to being in control. "Sure. Show me what you got to trade."

Dave shook his head. "Not the way I do business. My ass is freezing here. I want us to find someplace warm where we can sit down and do a trade properly. Not like a couple of robbers in a Western vid."

Something that might have been a laugh drifted out to them. "You an attorney in a previous life?"

"Accountant."

They heard a brief chortle. "Same difference, friend. Come through. Open up, Thad."

Bob Duvall was looking to stay comfortable in his spread. He'd been lucky in having a place with no back way in for rustlers and enough men and guns to keep it secure. He was in his early fifties, with a pale skin and even paler eyes.

"How many animals you got here?" Zera asked as they sat in front of a roaring fire, drinking something called Earl Grey tea.

"Around fifty trade horses. Three stallions and a dozen brood mares. Four... five mules."

"That's serious wealth," Dave said.

"And fifteen men and a shitload of firepower."

Next Dave asked about Sheever, describing the huge blond man to Duvall. "Didn't know his name. But it's the same guy, all right, on one of the finest stallions I ever saw. White as fresh milk."

"That's him. Did you trade with him?"

"Would've done. But he had some mean bastards with him, so I kept him the right side of my gates. He didn't much like that, but he didn't have enough men with him to make an issue of it."

"How many?" asked Lee.

Duvall considered. "Around seven or eight men and two girls."

"My daughters," said Dave.

The rancher nodded slowly. "And you need horses to get after him? You shouldn't have told me that, friend. Puts the price up real high."

Dave smiled pleasantly, then realized that Duvall wasn't joking. His jaw hardened, but he nodded. Chalk another one up for experience, he thought, but wasted no time on bitterness. "I'll remember that in future," he said.

"Business is business, friend."

Bob Duvall was as good as his word, driving a hard bargain over the animals Dave wanted. His ramrod, Thad, picked out three good horses for them, selecting the quietest of the pack mules.

"Think the boss is a hard bastard," he said to Dave, sensing his irritation at the high price.

"You could say that."

"There's another way of looking at it."

"What?"

Thad blew his nose into his glove and wiped it on the leg of his jeans. "All the men and guns he's got in the ranch... Easy to take what he wants and throw your corpses in the creek."

Dave looked at the man sideways. "I thought of that, too."

THE HEAVY GATE clanged shut behind them as they rode on just before noon. It was a relief not to have to carry the heavy packs. They also had fewer guns to take along.

Each still had a handgun. Dave the Linebaugh, Lee his 9 mm SIG-Sauer 232 and Zera the nickel-plated Ruger .32 that had belonged to Dave's dead wife, Janine.

One of the hunting bows was slung across the packs. Duvall had insisted on taking the scatter-guns, including Zera's beloved Smith & Wesson 3000. They still had one rifle, the Sauer 120 Lux with the Leupold optical sight.

Luckily Dave had not revealed the existence of the 15-round Skorpion machine pistol, leaving it hidden at the bottom of his pack, wrapped safely in the sleeping bag.

Duvall had also taken virtually all of their remaining food supplies. They'd augmented them from the kitchens of the late Widow Williams, but now they moved westward with only a few cans of stew and soup and a pack of jerky.

But he'd given them a sack of horse bones for the pit bull.

There was one other thing that Dave Rand had insisted on after the warnings he'd been given.

It was folded securely into his inside pocket. A bill of sale for the animals, dated and properly detailed and signed by Duvall.

In less than forty-eight hours that piece of paper was going to prove vital.

12

They rode higher, the air getting colder and thinner. At a bend in the highway there was a scenic turnoff, with amazing views across a hundred miles of mountains and valleys. Far behind them they could make out the region of intense volcanic activity, the sky smeared with dusty yellow clouds.

Ahead it seemed that they could nearly see clear over to the Pacific.

Horse droppings told them that they were almost certainly on the trail of Sheever, less than two days behind him.

It was an uneventful day, pushing on and trying to get used to their new mounts. Dave found it particularly difficult as the jolting seemed to make his jaw feel much more painful. By the time evening brought darkness, the inside of his thighs felt as though they'd been sandblasted.

"Getting old, Dad," said Lee as his father swung, painfully from the saddle.

"If getting old means having your ass and balls rubbed raw, then I'll just put a .475 through my head right now."

DURING THE NEXT MORNING, Lee, who was riding point, spotted hoof marks on a side trail. He reined in and called to the others.

"Riders going south," he said. "Lot of horses. Dozen or more."

Dave and Zera joined him, looking down at the trampled, frozen mud. "Sure this isn't Sheever and his gang, son?"

"Sure. Look. They carry on west. And these are fresher. Real recent."

MELMOTH GNAWED HAPPILY on his bones, cracking them with his enormously powerful jaws and lapping out the delicious marrow. He was virtually recovered from his mauling by the grizzly and kept up easily with the horses.

They'd stopped just before the middle of the day to rest the animals and take a trail snack. They were in a steep-sided valley that dipped between twin peaks, both layered in bright snow.

There was a quiet pool, fringed by dead bushes, where the horses and the mules could drink their fill, and a little dry grass for them to graze. The track was slippery and dangerous. Several times Dave had ordered a dismount to walk over the worst patches.

Lee had just stepped aside for a call of nature and rejoined the others, stopping and pointing at the pit bull. "Look. Melmoth's heard something."

"Hope it's not more bears," said Dave.

The dog didn't seem unduly worried, head lifted, staring back down the trail they'd just covered. Then, to Dave's concern, he looked the other way.

Ahead of them.

"Shit. Could be we're going to get some company. Listen."

"Horses," said Zera. "Over there...no, that way."

"Both," Lee said, reaching for his pistol.

But Dave checked him. "No. I can hear it. Got us caught in the middle. Sounds like at least twenty. Best play this one slow and careful. But if we have to move, then it's going to be fast."

"Keep our guns ready?"

"Right, Zera. All lie down and keep them tucked out of sight."

There wasn't that much time.

The noise of hooves and jingling harness came at a good lick. Bearing in mind the risks of going fast over the frozen mud, somebody was in a very serious hurry.

"Posse after us for what happened in Hope Springs?" Lee asked, breaking the silence between them.

"That was my first thought. But I don't see how anyone could've got ahead of us. Just wait and see and let me do the talking. Lee, leash up Melmoth quickly. Don't want him freaking out at whoever's coming."

The sound of the horsemen was very close.

First to arrive was the group who had been riding from the east. Dave lay still, not making any kind of threatening move, looking up at full twenty riders, led by a squat, muffled figure, face sheathed in layers of bright-colored scarves.

"Cover the fuckers!" The voice was a surprise. A thin, reedy, old woman's voice, the tones prim and formal, like a caricature of a maiden aunt.

Every one of the group was armed, with bandoliers of ammunition slung over shoulders. Most had hunting rifles, with a scattering of shotguns.

"Those horses yours, mister?"

Dave kept his cool. It wasn't for what had happened to the Widow Williams and her daughter. They were after rustlers.

"Yeah. And the mule."

"And I bet they got a bill of sale for 'em, Mrs. Fogarty!" shouted one of the men in the posse.

"All right if I reach in my pocket for it?" Dave asked.

The woman pulled a scarf away from her face, showing a sharp, beaklike nose and a mouth that seemed to have too many teeth brimming in it. "Slow and easy. When d'you buy them?"

"Yesterday mor—"

"No. Let the girl tell us."

Zera stood up very slowly, hands inside her parka. Dave knew that she was holding the .32-caliber Ruger.

"From a man named Bob Duvall. Yesterday morning. Took some of our best guns for them. The bastard drove a hard bargain because he knew we wanted them very badly."

"Watch your fucking tongue, girly," snapped the woman, managing to be both foulmouthed and prim at the same time. "Screwed you, did he? Sounds like that whoremonger, all right." She turned to Dave. "And you got a bill of sale, too. Best let me see it, mister."

He stood, followed by Lee, holding the snarling Melmoth on a tight lead.

At that moment the first of the other group of riders came spurring into the clearing, waving his hat and whooping.

"Caught 'em, Mrs. Fogarty!" Then he saw Dave, Zera and Lee standing at the wrong end of twenty guns. "Hey! You got three more?"

The woman reached out for Dave's fluttering piece of paper. For a dreadful moment he thought the rising wind might pluck it from her gloved fingers and whirl it away into the forest wilderness and within ten minutes all three of them would be hanged. But she held it. He noticed a silver-handled quirt dangling from her wrist, its leather thongs plaited with tiny wire knots.

"No," she called over her shoulder. "Looks like we got us the only three honest travelers in the whole state. Who've you caught?"

"Three. Reverend Huncke said to tell you one of them rode with the blond giant on the snow stallion."

"Sheever," Dave said.

Mrs. Fogarty finished reading the bill of sale and handed it back to him. "Looks fine to me. You said the name of Sheever, Mr. Rand. You know of him?"

"Personal reason for wanting to see him again. Prefer to leave it at that."

The woman nodded. "Your business. Best you take care in these parts." A thought struck her. "You're moving on west?"

"We are."

"Come and see how we deal with horse thieves around here."

"No. Thank you."

She smiled. "Wasn't precisely an invitation, Mr. Rand. I'd like you all to come, then you can pass the word as you ride on."

She gestured to his horses. "Mount up. Let's get to it."

Dave jerked his head at the others. "Sooner we do what she wants, then the quicker we can get on after Sheever. Let's go."

THERE WERE three prisoners.

When Mrs. Fogarty led her group up to the others, there were at least thirty-five in the posse. Bearing in mind how underpopulated the land was, Dave realized how seriously they took rustling.

In fact, it was just like a scene from an old western vid. The mounted posse, armed, wrapped against the biting cold. The dozen or so stolen ponies, and the three wretched people standing together under guard.

Dave sat on his chestnut mare, Zera on one side of him, Lee on the other. The pack mule was tethered behind them. To Melmoth's disgust, Lee had tied him to the stump of a long-dead sycamore.

A chubby man in a long black duster coat, sitting astride a spavined gelding, waved a welcome to their party. "In time to bid farewell to the ungodly, Mrs. Fogarty!" he shouted.

"Glad to see you got the miserable bastards, Reverend Huncke," she replied.

Dave looked at the three prisoners. One was an old man with a tobacco-stained beard. He kept staring at the ground and shuffling his feet. Like the other two, he had his hands tied behind him with a length of hemp rope.

The second was a woman. She wore a torn felt hat, pulled down over her eyes, and it was difficult to tell her age. A necklace of cheap plastic beads was strung around her throat. Even from twenty paces away, Dave was aware that she was possibly the filthiest, smelliest person he had ever seen in his life.

The third of the trio was different.

He was short and skinny, wearing a thermal army jacket and pants. His head was bare, showing a stubble of iron-gray hair. There was an old jagged scar around his right eye, as though someone had once broken a bottle end in his face. He had been staring out over the mountains when the second group arrived, and he didn't turn around to look at them.

Lee touched his father on the arm. "That's the one," he said. "Think he was called Lemuel. One of the sort of lieutenants to Sheever."

The setting was staggeringly beautiful. There was a frozen lake to their left, with a distant waterfall smoking with icy spray. A small island stuck up from the rippled expanse of gray, like a ghost ship upon a spectral ocean. Mountains crowded all around, snow topped, with white streaking their flanks. The sky was clear from east to west, shimmering with the palest blue.

Mrs. Fogarty heeled her horse forward to the front. She looked at the prisoners. "Any of you got anything to say before we hang you?"

The woman turned slowly and looked up at her. Dave saw the face of an imbecile, totally lacking any expression, snot clogged around her nose, dirt encrusted in the furrows by the mouth.

"You." Mrs. Fogarty pointed at her with the quirt. "Anything to say?"

"Fuck you for a drink."

"I'll put that offer on the back burner, thank you. Nothing else to say about the horses?"

The blank, dead eyes blinked twice. The woman moved her feet slightly, the dulled stare not changing. They heard the sound of tinkling water, and a pool of liquid appeared between the muddied boots, spreading into the frozen earth.

"Jesus Christ," someone said disgustedly.

The old man looked up and walked toward Mrs. Fogarty, his lips worked feebly.

"Speak up!"

He was pressed right against the flank of her horse. Dave was close by but he couldn't hear a word. Mrs. Fogarty leaned from the saddle, then straightened, shaking her head. "Can't hear a blind fucking word he's mumbling!"

"I said you wasn't to kill me. Wasn't my fault. Didn't know what we was doing. Me and the woman was doing fine, then he came and made us do all the stealing."

Everyone looked toward Lemuel. He shrugged his shoulders, still affecting an interest in the surrounding landscape.

The Reverend Huncke was near him and called out, "You got anything to tell us?"

Behind him, the old man had fallen into a servile crouch, trying to kiss Mrs. Fogarty's riding boots. She lashed out at him with the whip, the tip catching him on the side of the face and opening a ragged weal from which blood began to flow.

He dropped to his knees and began to weep.

Lemuel sniffed. "Man could have better company to die in," he said.

Reverend Huncke beamed delightedly. "Prefer to hang a thief with some gumption," he said, and laughed.

"Get on with it," said Lemuel. "You can only do it once."

"Fair comment. Get the ropes up and put them on horses."

The old man, still crying, was hauled to his feet and a noose looped around his neck. The woman stood still while they adjusted the rope about her throat, pulling the long knot in behind her left ear. Lemuel feinted to kick at the men who came to tie him, laughing delightedly as they all backed off.

"Cowardly bunch of shits," he said quietly. He stood patiently while he was lifted astride one of the horses. The other end of the rope was tied off around the bole of the hanging-tree.

He looked around him, his eyes passing Zera, Dave and Lee, then returning to Lee again.

"He's recognized me, Dad," said the boy.

On an impulse Dave heeled his horse to the front, pushing some of the posse aside. "Lemuel," he said.

"Shut up, Mr. Rand," said the spinsterish Mrs. Fogarty.

"I want to ask this man some questions."

"I don't want to talk to him," Sheever's lieutenant said. "Don't know him. Never seen him before." His eyes went back to Lee, and then he smiled. "Oh, well... Maybe I do know you after all."

The Reverend Huncke glowered at Dave. "Don't know you, mister... but time's passing and these three have an appointment with their Maker. And we don't want them to be late, do we?"

"I need to talk."

Lemuel smiled crookedly. "Seems a touch late, Mr. Rand."

"Where's Sheever going?"

"West."

"Where?"

Mrs. Fogarty was at Dave's side, lifting the tip of her quirt and planting a feathered touch on his cheek with it. "No time. We need to set them dangling," she said, sounding like a school librarian announcing that they'd be closing in five minutes.

"Five minutes," Dave pleaded.

She shook her head, turning to the three bound figures on the held horses. "Not even five seconds."

Dave caught Lemuel's eyes. "Tell me about my daughters!" he shouted.

"Drop them!" called Mrs. Fogarty.

The small man cracked his stubbled face into a vicious grin. "You won't see 'em again. But if you ever do, they won't never be like they was."

"Why?" asked Dave, conscious as he spoke that he was too late.

The horses were slapped on the hindquarters, making them start forward. The old man and the half-witted woman both slipped off easily, but Lemuel fought for a few more seconds of life, trying to grip the animal with his knees.

"Mistake," someone said.

In the breathless stillness, there was the clear brittle crack of the old man's neck snapping. The woman strangled quickly, spinning around, legs kicking for twenty seconds or so. She gave a gargling, choking cry, and then was still.

Lemuel died harder. He'd flexed the muscles of his neck, so that the rope failed to break it. Because he was strong and wiry, it took a long time for him to strangle to death.

The posse watched him in silence, some men leaning forward on their pommels, some looking away from the hideous spectacle.

"Someone hang on his legs," said Reverend Huncke, but nobody moved.

"Thou shalt not keep a thief from suffering, Reverend," said Mrs. Fogarty, her head angled eagerly toward the swinging, thrashing body.

Lemuel's eyes looked as though they were going to burst from their sockets and dangle on his purpled cheeks. His tongue was blackened, blood speckling it. The arms were rigid as he strained against the bindings.

Dave closed his eyes, not liking the sight nor Mrs. Fogarty's enjoyment of it.

"That's enough," he said. Drawing the Linebaugh, he steadied it and put a single booming round through the hanging man's head.

Blood and brains and sharp splinters of bone dappled the men all around Lemuel. The noise of the handgun made several of the horses rear and kick.

"Shouldn't have done that, Mr. Rand," Mrs. Fogarty said quietly.

13

Sheever was in a vile, bloody rage.

When he was unsaddling his stallion at dusk, the horse turned and snapped at him, catching him in the forearm with its sharp, tombstone teeth. The yellow-haired giant pulled free and then delivered a stunning punch to the horse's face, striking it just above the rolling eye and sending it tottering to its knees. He kicked the animal several times before walking stiff-legged away from it.

Though they were never included in any of the conversations around the night fires, Ellie and Roxanne couldn't avoid knowing that things were going badly for the group.

Over the months they'd been held by Sheever, the numbers had fallen steadily. One by one, men dropped out. Not many were still living when they dropped out. Sheever wasn't too hot on allowing that to happen. Some had died of sickness. Cholera and typhoid were common. Two had chilled themselves, three if they counted the man they'd found in a deep pool one morning with no mark of violence on him.

There had been several deaths as a direct or indirect result of fights.

Some had run away. Most had been caught. That was another thing that Sheever didn't much like.

One had been thrown from his horse on a steep trail. The girls would never forget how he'd screamed all the way down for such a long, long time.

About six others had simply been killed by Sheever.

Now little Lemuel hadn't returned from his mission to obtain some more horses for the survivors.

And Sheever was in a vile, bloody rage.

"I SOMETIMES WONDER if it's worth going on."

Dave looked across at the young woman. There was a thick mist hanging about the high valleys, and he'd decided it was worth the chance of detection to light a fire for the night.

"After the girls, you mean?"

Zera ran her fingers through her matted blond hair and sighed. "No, not that. Just...I guess I'm thinking about the 'meaning of life' sort of thing."

Lee nodded. He was sitting against a moss-covered tree stump, rubbing a dozing Melmoth under the chin. "I know what you mean. It's got so that I lie awake at night and I just try and remember what living was like before the big impact." He turned to his father. "Couple of nights ago...I couldn't sleep and I started thinking about home. Highridge Canyon Road, Cody Heights. And about Mom."

"What about her?"

Lee put a hand to his eyes, and his voice was trembling. "*Nothing* about her, Dad. That's the whole bastard point. I couldn't even remember her face, her voice. Nothing!"

"It's hard for each of us, son. But just think what it's like for your sisters."

"Least they're probably safe, Dave," said Zera. "If he was going to do anything crucial with them, he'd have done it by now."

SHEEVER BROKE a thick piece of wood between his fingers and threw it onto the fire, then glanced around him at the swirling fog. All six of his surviving gang were with him, discussing how they could get more horses and more food.

"All right," said the massive figure of Sheever in his quiet grating voice. He hadn't shaved for several days and now wore a silvery beard and mustache. "All right. First chance we get, I'll offer the girls for trading. Sell them for animals or supplies. Everyone agree with that?" There was a long silence. "Well, nobody disagrees."

THOUGH IT WAS still late December and they were up in the high country, the weather tilted through one of its radical changes. They went to bed, wrapped in thermal clothes and tucked into sleeping bags, resigned to having ice on their faces and laced around their eyes when they woke.

Long before dawn they were out of the bags, peeling off layers of clothes, soaked in sweat from the abrupt rise in temperature.

The trees around were weeping like a convention of widows, snow melting and ice dripping. The ground had gone from rippled iron to shifting mud, and a thick fog had come from the west, reducing visibility to less than ten paces. A quarter of an hour later it was less than five paces.

"What's going on?" said Lee, trying to pack his gear away in misty blackness. "You don't reckon it's something to do with a volcano or hot springs or something like that? Do you, Dad?"

"No. We'd have heard eruptions or smelled the stink of it. I reckon it's just a variation on the freakish weather we've had for the last year or so."

"But it's sweltering."

Dave shook his head. "Can't argue with that, son. If we still had books of records, I reckon this could qualify. Must have gone from minus thirty to plus thirty in about three hours."

Zera sniffed. "The air's keying strange. Smells so green and moist, like the inside of a botanical garden. Won't this mean there'll be floods along the trail, lover?"

"Have to see. Make the going hard. I've been thinking about Lemuel . . . the one they hanged."

"What about him?"

Dave could barely see the face of the young woman as he spoke to her. "He was after horses. For himself? Or for Sheever? Either way he never got any. It just *might* mean that they're short of animals. Weather like this'll only make it worse."

"But he might not be short of horses," Lee said. "Then what?"

Dave picked his way carefully across to start saddling his own mare. "I guess it doesn't make much difference really."

By the time they were packed and saddled, there was a hint of gray light seeping through the fog. But visibility was still less than twenty paces.

"How're we going to track them through this?" Lee questioned his father.

"Slowly. But at least we know they're on this trail. Watch hard for side turns and check them. Sheever might suspect we're following him. But enough time's past for him to start feeling more relaxed. That means careless. Gives us the edge we need."

Melmoth hated the fog. It seemed to smother the pit bull, cowing him. He skulked at the heels of the last horse, his head turning unhappily from side to side. The swathing mist blurred his fine-tuned senses, throwing him on the defensive.

Dave led the way, allowing his mare to pick her path and pace. Loose stones shifted under hooves, and narrow streams trickled all about them.

The temperature was still rising, and water dripped noisily from the branches of the trees. Dave whistled between his teeth, running a finger round his collar to try to cool himself a little.

"Can't believe this muggy heat," he called behind to Zera, who was riding second.

"Anything in the map that might give a clue where Sheever's going?"

"Not really. Town about ten miles west of here, across a river. Place called Romero Springs."

"Big?"

Dave shook his head, flicking water from his hair. "No. Sounds like a resort town. There's some kind of entertainment complex shown in thin red type. Looks like a zoo or something."

"Doesn't sound like the kind of place Sheever might hole up in."

"Who knows, Zera? Who knows?"

A watery sun finally made its belated appearance just before the middle of the day, breaking through the suffocating cloud cover and beginning to burn off the mist.

A light breeze sprang up from the southwest, blowing away the last tattered shreds of the fog, bringing freshness and the promise of a beautiful December afternoon.

"I can't believe that it's just after Christmas and here we are in the northwest, pouring sweat." Dave laughed. "Can't believe it."

"You think that life might ever get back...the weather and everything...to what it was before? Only, I wonder sometimes whether the Earth might have been pushed off its axis."

Dave looked over his shoulder at his son. "I don't think we'd ever know, Lee. Can't look it up in *Scientific American* or anything like that."

Zera heeled her horse forward, joining Dave on the widening trail. "Lover?"

"What?"

"After... What then?"

"After what? Oh, you mean when we've rescued Ellie and Roxanne?"

"Yeah."

He didn't answer her for several long seconds. Finally he said, "I truly don't know, Zera. If you're asking me about us..."

"I think I am, Dave."

"I think...I think we should talk about this after, not now. There's just too many imponderables to muddy the water right now."

"But you think maybe?"

He smiled at her, feeling a sudden swelling of emotion for the young woman. "Yeah, lover. I think maybe."

Evening came as they were negotiating a steep, winding bridle path. There'd been a couple of carved markers to show hiking trails. They had indicated that Romero Springs was only about eight miles away from them.

Since the intermediate points shown were Double Eagle Falls and Brooke Ridge, it seemed a fair guess that they would be going down and then up again.

"Best camp before dark, Dad?"

Dave reined in and stood in the stirrups. There was a thickening fog appearing in elusive rags between the trees ahead of them.

"Maybe we'll go down into the bottom of the valley, then camp."

Lee whistled. "Hey! Listen to that noise. Like thunder."

"Must be the Double Eagle Falls. The way the snow and ice has been melting today, they could be kind of big."

IT WAS A GOOD SITE for camping, except for the pounding roar of the waterfall. A clearing just off the trail, with a stream surging through it, emptying itself into the foaming falls. The fog hung over the rainbowed spray, making it safe to risk a fire.

"If the mist clears, then we should put the fire out," Zera suggested.

"Yeah. And I think we'd best post a watch, with Sheever being close to us."

The horses were tethered to a rope knotted between a pair of lodgepole pines. Dave had worried the animals hadn't been getting enough food, but the rapid thaw had revealed fresh fodder under the melting snow, and water wasn't a problem.

"Me first on watch?" Lee offered.

"Why not? But I'd like us to stay up reasonably late. Cuts the time alone that way."

For the first time in weeks they would have a problem trying to find some dry wood for the fire. Everything was wet, the trunks of trees slick with melted snow. But Lee managed to scrape at the packed leaf mold with the point of his Mamba Blackjack, uncovering layers that were dust-dry.

The flames were soon licking brightly at some broken branches, hissing at the occasional patch of dampness on them.

A few cans of stew were soon bubbling over the fire, sending their rich, artificial scent through the forest.

"I'm tired," said Zera. "When I was a little girl, I used to think that there was nothing nicer than the idea of a great powerful beast thrusting between my thighs."

"And now?" Lee asked daringly, smirking as he picked up on her joke.

She leaned forward and patted him on the cheek. "There's times I still like the idea of it. But I'm not so keen on horses anymore."

DAVE AND HIS SON sat together in the humid night, each cradling a mug of something that was called coffee and wasn't. Zera was sleeping soundly a few feet away from them. She lay on her side, the top of the bag pushed back.

Lee saw his father look toward the young woman. "You love her, Dad?"

The question took Dave by surprise. "Love...? I truly don't know. I loved your mother once, Lee. And I can't recall what the feeling was really like. I know there was a time when my heart leapt just at the sight of her and that when...if we went out, there was nobody in the entire universe that I'd rather be with."

"But things weren't going so well, were they? Ellie and me used to talk about it."

"About what?" His eye was caught by one of the horses. It had suddenly stiffened and was standing with its head turned toward the north, ears flattening back.

"If you and Mom got divorced. Who we'd go to live with and all... Hey, look at Melmoth."

The dog had stood up, his muzzle drilling northward, lips peeling back off the razored teeth. There was a deep, rumbling snarl beginning in his belly. The one ear was pricked.

"I can't hear anything over the noise of the falls," Dave said as he stood up, his hand dropping to the walnut butt of the Linebaugh.

Now all three of the horses were showing signs of extreme discomfort. One tossed its head and whinnied, trying to rear up.

The noise woke Zera. She fumbled her way out of the sleeping bag and went to join the others. "What the...?" she began.

"Something out there," Lee said, his voice raised over the pounding of the water.

"What?"

Dave started to move in the direction of the spooked animals, his gun already drawn. "Bears is my guess. Better get ready for them."

It wasn't bears.

Melmoth started to bark, high and angry, overlaid with something almost unprecedented. Fear.

It wasn't bears.

If it had just been bears, it wouldn't have been so bad.

14

"Dad! Look out!"

Dave had gone to try to gentle the horses, but even as he reached them he realized that it was already way too late. At Lee's screamed warning, he flung himself back and sideways, hearing the sharp humming sound as the taut rope snapped under the animals' terror.

Hooves pounded near and over him as he curled himself into a ball, head in his arms. Moments later the clearing only held Zera, Lee, Melmoth and himself. The horses and the pack mule were gone, swallowed into the wilderness. The noise of their passing was disappearing under the roaring of Double Eagle Falls.

"You all right?" Zera shouted, rushing to his side and stooping by him.

"I'm fine, but we've lost the fucking horses!"

"Maybe they'll come back."

"They were off their heads. Chances are they'll run all the way back to Duvall's ranch!"

"What spooked 'em like that?" Lee asked, now hanging on with both hands to Melmoth's leash. The pit bull was straining against it, a whitish froth dangling from his jaws.

"Whatever it is, we better get ready. From the way the animals were scenting, it looks like it's coming from the north. Down toward the falls."

"Shall we go look?"

"It's open down there. Least we should be able to make out what's coming." Seeing how difficult Melmoth was becoming, Dave told Lee to let him take the dog. "Get your pistol out."

"Shouldn't you leave Melmoth here?" Zera added worriedly.

"No. I'd have to tie him, and then whatever it is might come up behind and waste him before we could get back to help. Better we keep him by us." Leaning down, he cuffed the pit bull across the side of the head. "Keep quiet!" he snapped.

The sky had cleared, and the thin column of smoke from their fire rose almost vertically to the tops of the trees around, then the wind snatched at it and tore it to rags.

Apart from an almost inaudible protesting whine from Melmoth, the night was very still.

"Too quiet," Dave whispered as they made their way toward the river.

"What?" said Zera.

"I said it's too quiet." He grinned at her. "But let it pass."

An animal shot out from the north side of the trail, running fast, head down, tongue out, making them jump.

"What was that?"

"Wolf, I think. In a hurry."

Suddenly Dave was aware of movement all around them, as though the woods had come to a secret, bustling life. Nothing showed itself, but the undergrowth crackled and stirred.

Zera was in the lead and she halted, turning toward Dave, her face a white blur in the filtered moonlight. "I really don't fucking like this, lover."

He could feel the short hairs at the nape of his neck beginning to rise stiffly. His palms were moist with sweat, and he licked his dry lips. "Don't much like it, either. But it's better to face it rather than have it creepy-crawl around behind us."

Now they were right by the twin falls.

The noise was deafening, making conversation almost impossible. A trail came toward them from the north, snaking to the left about fifty yards from them, so it was impossible to see if anything was coming that way. Farther beyond them the trail had been undercut by a quake and vanished into the foaming spray of the river. A maze of tumbled and broken pines was locked together, forming a spectral, frail bridge over the waterfall. Its skeletal silhouette disappeared at its high point into the silvery mist.

Now the rush of movement had finished, ended as abruptly as it had started.

Melmoth had begun to pull at the lead again as they reached the bottom of the path. He struggled to go toward the north, toward the blind bend in the main trail. Now, as Dave gazed around, the brindled dog shook his head, as if something was bothering his hearing.

"What's wrong, boy?"

The dog looked up at him, as if he were seeking some kind of reassurance. Then he took two steps back and pressed his flank against Dave's boots, very slowly lowering himself to the wet earth, belly down.

Dave reached to pat him and found that he was trembling.

Fear from Melmoth was something he'd never encountered, and it made his own blood run slow and chill. If the pit bull was that frightened...

"Keep together," he shouted. "Close!"

He stared into the lake of shadow that swamped the corner of the northern trail, keeping it in darkness.

"There's something there, under the trees," yelled Lee.

"Like a carpet or..." Zera said, slowly starting to back up.

Dave recognized it first.

"Rats!"

Boiling along the trail like a horrendous biblical visitation. From God knew where—some apocalyptic midnight pit—the rats were moving. Tens of thousands of them. Lean, gray, ruby eyed in the moonlight. The scratching of their claws rose over the thunder of Double Eagle Falls.

Dave's analytical mind forced itself above the mute horror of the moment.

Options. Try to fight or scare them? Ludicrous against an army.

Run? Where? There could be other battalions of the rodents, sliding like an endless ribbon of murderous gray velvet through the forest.

"Keep still!" he bellowed. "Keep very still. It's our only hope."

The first of the rats were only a few paces from them, heads going up, noses sniffing at the intruders.

Melmoth came to sudden life, onto his feet, the beginning of a barking, suicidal rage swelling in his throat. Dave felt it rather than heard it and reacted without a second's hesitation. He swung the barrel of the Linebaugh hard across the pit bull's head, knocking him cold. Then he bent to scoop him up from under the whiskers of the advance guard of the vermin army.

He had a moment for one last warning to Zera and Lee. "Stay still," he said. He wasn't sure whether they even heard him.

Then the rats were on them, around them, swarming all over them.

Dave hugged the unconscious body of Melmoth to him, closing his own eyes and mouth, trying to breathe as lightly and shallowly as possible.

He felt the scampering bodies, their tiny claws hooking into his clothes as they scaled his legs and stomach, then across his chest. Some of them quickly reached his face.

He was aware of a strange smell. Dry, like powdered straw that prickled at his nose and throat. Like the inside of a derelict barn.

Cool noses poked at the skin of his face, probing delicately, inquisitively at him, pushing at his closed lips, at the lids of his quivering eyes. Silent, alien breath on his skin. He felt Melmoth stir, and his own heart leapt in his chest. Part of his brain functioned well enough to tell him to leap to a whirling death in the falls rather than die where he stood among that armada of snapping death.

Time passed, slithered by him like the rustling progress of an infinitely large and ancient cobra.

He felt the weight of hundreds of tiny bodies scurrying about him.

Gradually the weight diminished, as one by one the rats lost interest in this strange warm statue. They scampered back down him, onto the streaming earth.

Seconds...or minutes...later, Dave Rand finally opened his eyes. The rats were gone, leaving only the trees and the rumbling waters and the moonlight.

Melmoth was coming around, making a coughing sound in his throat. Zera was a few steps away, her face like parchment, trying for a smile.

Lee was on the other side, eyes wide open, looking at his father with a desperate intensity. "That was interesting, Dad!" he shouted, then promptly fainted.

15

All they had now were the clothes on their backs, a sleeping bag and a handgun for each, along with the bow and a quiver of arrows Dave had taken before the pack mule had fled.

The food supplies were gone.

"I should have unloaded the animal," he said as they sat around the last glowing ashes of their fire, recovering from the ordeal. "But there wasn't very much, and I always figure we can move fast if we have to. Well, that old mule moved fucking fast enough."

"Now what?" said Lee, hugging his knees to his chest. He'd come around quickly after passing out, and nobody had mentioned it.

"Now we climb up over Brooke Ridge as soon as there's a touch of dawn. Should be able to see Romero Springs from there—and maybe find Sheever and the girls. I have a feeling the chase is ending."

THEY CROSSED a highway on the way up to the top of the climb. A crumbling blacktop. A sign, warning that the bridge froze before the pavement. Bullet holes peppered the sign. Dave stood and looked at it, feeling a pang of nostalgia for the world that had gone forever. If he concentrated on that sign, he could imagine that he and Janine and the kids were on a hiking vacation up in Washington State.

"Daydreaming, Dad?" Lee called from the other side of the road, bringing him back with a jolt to consider their new situation.

Melmoth had a lump on the side of his head the size of a quail's egg, but it didn't seem to slow him down. He scampered along ahead of them, barking as he put up some duck from a small beaver-lake.

Dave regretted the loss of their hunting rifle in the night. Food was going to be that much more difficult to kill with only handguns, limited ammunition and the bow.

On the way up the hill he suddenly felt tired. Old and tired. The anticipation of finally closing on his nemesis brought home to him what a strange and bloody road it had been.

When the asteroid had crashed to Earth, it hadn't just meant the end of civilization on the broadest scale. It had meant irrevocable change for every survivor.

Those who didn't change were not going to be survivors.

Lee was first to the top of the ridge, leaning his hand on a single lightning-scarred cedar and waving back to the others to join him.

"It's a big valley, and I can see Romero Springs. Doesn't look very big. Shopping mall and...hey, there's a kind of flooding around the place."

Dave was right there in a second, Zera at his heels. He took several deep breaths, relishing the freshness of the day as he looked out across an amazing view.

Romero Springs lay at the bottom of a bowl, with snow-topped peaks encircling it. A river ran through the town, but it must have been blocked by an earth shift, because water was backing up across the floor of the valley. Far beneath where they stood looking down, the river had already formed a lake.

"Jesus!" Zera exclaimed.

"What?"

"Be a shitload of meltwater coming down the pike after this rise in temperature. Day or so, and the whole valley's going to be one huge lake."

Dave had lost the binoculars along with the pack mule, and he now shaded his eyes and stared down, looking for signs of life. But they were too high above the settlement to make out any movement.

"Shopping mall's on the high side of the town," Lee observed.

"Be worth a visit."

"What about Sheever?" asked Zera.

"If he's anywhere, it could be up by that mall. Just have to walk slow and watch fast."

IT WAS a difficult and hazardous hike down the side of the mountain toward the valley floor.

The occasional small rivulet had become a frothing, murderous torrent. Streams had become rivers. The weird, unseasonal temperature rise had melted ice and snow clear across the region. Water now flowed over the earth, carrying years of leaf mold with it, making every step slippery and perilous.

Melmoth hated it, picking his way through the slime and mud, sometimes falling. On one occasion his paws went away from him, and he slid more than a hundred feet down the slope, creating a bow wave of watery mud. But when they finally caught up with him, the pit bull seemed no worse for the experience.

The lower they came, the more they could see of the effects of the flooding.

The narrow neck of the valley, which had been directly below them, had carried a two-lane blacktop, now submerged. That was where the earth shift had struck, blocking off the entire mouth of the valley to a depth of better than three hundred feet. Packed dirt and rock and shattered trees.

"Can't see how deep it is," said Dave. "Too much light off the surface."

Lee pointed to a side road, lined with neat frame houses, running down into the nature-made lake.

"Way they go down, it looks like it's at least fifty feet deep at the end there."

"Could be."

"What happens when the water gets toward the top of that dam?" asked Zera.

"Then anyone living the other side of it should get ready to run. Far and fast and high."

The convex shape of the hillside meant that they couldn't see what lay at the bottom of the trail until they were nearly all the way down.

The rest of the valley and small township of Romero Springs had opened up, with the rectangular block of the shopping mall now clearly visible. But still they spotted no sign of life.

"Hey, look here," Zera called, picking her way cautiously through the deepening mud at the front.

Dave was behind her and he stopped, hanging on to the damp trunk of a sturdy aspen. Lee, bringing up the rear, cursed under his breath as his boots slipped and he nearly fell.

Melmoth, panting, his brindled color now coated light brown, waited patiently.

In front of them was the rusted remains of a high, heavy-gauge wire fence. The sections that remained showed it once rose to at least twenty feet in height, topped with a triple layer of razored bars, and what looked like an electrified strand, its porcelain conductors dangling loose. They rattled softly in the breeze.

"Prison?" suggested Lee.

"Could be. But there's no sign of any watchtowers nearby, and there's trees and all sorts of vegetation in there. Also some buildings." Dave sniffed. "No. Doesn't look like a prison to me."

"Shall we go ahead? Or try and find a way around it?"

"Straight ahead," Dave replied. "Whatever it used to be . . . won't be that now."

Before they reached the first of the buildings, they stumbled over a corpse, or what remained of a corpse.

Only the skull, with a few strands of brown hair pasted flat to the bone, showed that it had ever been a human being. The rest of it was a tangled assortment of scattered bones, some held together with shreds of stringy gristle.

"Boy," whistled Lee. "Someone did a good job on him."

"Could be her," Zera remarked.

"Doesn't much matter now." Dave pushed at the skull with the toe of his boot. It rolled over in the long, wet grass, disturbing a turquoise beetle that skittered away. "Could have died of anything. Scavengers . . . coyotes or wolves, or dogs, did this."

There were parts of another skeleton close by, this time without any sign of a skull.

Zera touched Dave's arm. "Don't think it was some kind of research lab, do you?"

"What? Nerve warfare? Chemical stuff like they used to stockpile in the nineties? Suppose it might be."

"Could go round, Dad."

Dave paused, noticing that Melmoth wasn't looking too happy, his head turning from side to side as he scented the air.

"What's up, boy?"

"He can smell something. Maybe it's old chemical poisons," Zera said.

Dave sniffed, trying to catch a hint of what was bothering the pit bull. There seemed to be the faintest trace of an ammoniac sourness that was reminiscent of urine-soaked straw in an old stable.

"We'll carry on, but be careful. I'll go ahead."

The nearest of the concrete buildings was only a few cautious paces ahead of them, with an acacia bush standing dead and dry by a green iron door.

"Hold the dog, Lee. Don't come in immediately. Just wait and keep a lookout."

He reached out and opened the door, using the heavy sliding bolt. The air was cold and damp and very musty. The door was on drop hinges. Its weight pulled itself from his hands, slamming shut and leaving him in semidarkness.

Dave turned quickly around, drawing the Linebaugh. Then he saw something only ten feet away from him. A rhinoceros!

For a heart-stopping, gripping moment, Dave Rand thought that he was about to die. His next momentary thought was that the rhinoceros was a statue. But his eyes told him it wasn't.

A second and more careful glance revealed the truth to him.

It was a rhinoceros, but it was a dead rhinoceros.

When the others joined him, they stood around, looking on in wonder.

"Must've starved," said Zera. "That's keying sad."

The animal had simply fallen to its side and died there, looking like a discarded winter overcoat, gray, ponderous and massively wrinkled. Locked away in its sarcophagus, the wretched creature had not been touched by predators. Its eyes and some of the soft tissues around its mouth had rotted away completely, and the stone floor around it was stained with the dried remnants of its bodily fluids.

Now it lay there, its horn tilted dejectedly to one side.

"At least we know that this isn't a chemical warfare base," Dave said. "Unless they were using ground rhino's horn for some sort of mystic purpose."

Lee had gone out through the door on the far side of the enclosure and returned to report what he'd found.

"Kind of safari park. Seems deserted. Certainly no sign of any people around. The low ground's already flooded."

Dave looked once more at the melancholy relic of the dead rhino. "Yeah, well . . . let's go and see what other surprises Romero Springs has to offer."

The meltwater was flooding into the upper end of the wide valley from the high mountains faster than Dave would have believed possible. The level of the lake seemed to be rising even as they stood and looked at it. Out in the open, they could now see clearly the shape of the wildlife park.

The rear area, where the rhino house stood, was pressed into the flank of the hill, and had held some of the larger creatures. Most of the buildings were closed, and Dave could see no reason to investigate them.

"Just going to be a mess of dead animals. I'd rather not see that."

Nearer the entrance there had been an area where people could drive their cars through an open space. Dave had once visited a place like it on a trip to Montreal. Separate sections had housed the lions and the bears, and a stretch of land allowed the baboons to run riot. He had a vivid memory of one of them tugging on the wiper while urinating on the windshield from a curiously pink penis. A day later they'd also found a heap of baboon droppings on the top of the car.

"Wonder if any of the animals got away?" said Lee. "Lot of the fences are down."

Dave looked around. The outer wall was fractured in a number of places, presumably from the earth movements in the aftermath of Adastreia. And, as his son had pointed out, whole lengths of the retaining fences had simply vanished.

"If the rhinoceros is anything to go by, most of the dangerous ones were penned in."

"Dead giraffe there," Zera said, gesturing toward a heap of bones and mottled skin in one corner of the open area. "This is awful. Poor thing."

The remains reminded Dave of a visit to the La Brea Tar Pits. The skeletal reconstructions of the long-necked dinosaurs were oddly like the jumbled bones of the giraffe.

"That's the reptile house over there," Lee observed.

"Sounds like a good place to avoid. Snakes can survive an awfully long time. Wouldn't want to walk in on a bunch of hungry rattlers."

Melmoth was subdued, walking patiently on his leash, as though Lee were taking him downtown to pick up the magazines.

Dave had taken point, making his way carefully through long grass, his eyes sweeping from side to side. He was absurdly conscious that he was really looking out for a lion or a tiger creeping up on him. But the bizarre heat and humidity did make it all feel a little like cutting trail through an equatorial jungle.

There was a souvenir stall to the right of the overgrown path, its window shattered, a dozen boxes of film on the concrete around it. A black-and-yellow sign arrowed the way in the direction of the restaurant and children's play area. Another notice was headed Feeding Times. Beneath that it was completely blank.

The path began to zigzag downhill, and Dave saw the glint of water. The sound of the river reached his ears, growing louder and angrier.

"Could be a problem, people," he said over his shoulder.

The water had already reached into the lowest part of the safari park, flooding the entrance gates and the ticket booths. It was around eighteen inches deep, but it was visibly rising, creeping up with an infinite slowness. It seemed infinitely slow until they looked away for a couple of minutes and found it had gone up another inch or so.

"If we're going to get up the hill toward the shopping mall, I think we'd better start right now," Dave said.

He wished he'd still had the Nikon glasses. It would have been an enormous help to know in advance if Sheever was really holed up in Romero Springs. Also, he'd want to take a good look higher up the valley to try to gauge the conditions with the huge quantities of melted ice and snow pouring through.

"Looks like it's deeper just across the highway there," said Lee.

"Dammit to hell!" Dave shook his head. "We should have kept to the higher ground. Now we have to go all the way back and around or try and pick our way through what lies ahead."

The main river was to the left, with its flooded overflow running directly across in front of them.

"Let's wade it." Zera grinned. "Could do with a bath."

"And with this warm weather, there's no risk of hypothermia, Dad."

"All right. But carry Melmoth, Lee. If he gets washed away, we'll not have much chance of ever finding him again."

DAVE TOOK a sudden, sharp breath. "Jeeeeesus!" The day was so hot and sticky that the meltwater felt like a hundred below. It just reached to his knees, but he was already aware of the power as it tugged at him.

"What a lot of fuss, Dave," Zera teased, but she also pulled an agonized face as she entered the edge of the water.

Lee was holding Melmoth in his arms, and the pit bull was struggling half-heartedly.

There was a wall angling across in front of them, and it created a pool of turbulence, the water moving in odd, flat slabs. By now it was over Dave's knees, and he was having serious second thoughts about the crossing. The ground was fairly even under his feet, but it was still difficult to keep his balance.

He half turned, arms out to avoid falling, trying to hoist the bow and quiver higher on his shoulders. "Everyone okay, or do we go back?" he shouted.

Zera gave him a wobbly thumbs-up. Behind her, Lee nodded and grinned. "So far, so good, Dad!" he yelled.

Dave pressed on, into a patch of slightly calmer water in the lee of the wall. Immediately beyond it, the flow was much quicker, but it also looked more shallow.

"Seems easier after this!"

Then he saw the first of the snakes.

It was a mere swirl and flurry in the dark water a couple of paces ahead of him. Then he caught a glimpse of a long, scaled body, looking as thick around as his upper arm.

He stopped dead. As his hand fumbled for the Linebaugh on his hip, he saw a second reptile, this time a shovel-shaped head and tiny black eyes. A darting mouth appeared, pale against the rest of the body.

Dave took a breath to warn the others and found his voice had been shocked into silence. He swallowed and tried again.

Suddenly there wasn't any need for any warning. All around the three of them the water started to boil with dozens of poisonous cottonmouths.

Dave lost his footing and went under, his mouth filling with the icy flood, his mind screamingly aware of sinuous, twining bodies all about him.

17

It was the one and only time in his entire life that Dave Rand ever totally surrendered to panic.

The horrific nightmare of his situation freaked him out to such an extent that he had no idea what he was doing. He had absolutely no control over what was going on.

Someone was screaming and choking, and he had no idea that it was himself.

At one point he had a snake in his hands, holding it near the throat, and he jerked at it, snapping the spine, then blindly pushing the flailing corpse away from him.

He scrambled over the wall, scraping his knuckles, flopping over into the faster, less deep water on the far side. He landed on his face, inhaling mouthfuls from the freezing river and nearly choking himself again. Finally he struggled upright in water that reached just above his knees.

He was still gripping the heavy pistol. There was a pain in his right wrist, as though he'd nearly dislocated it, and to his bewilderment Dave realized that he'd fired the Linebaugh. But he didn't know when or at what.

Now he fought the panic. Closing his eyes for a moment, he heaved in several short, juddering breaths. He slowed his breathing forcibly and opened his eyes, looking behind him over the wall.

Zera was away to the right, upstream, holding her hunting knife in her right hand, staring intently into the water. Another few steps, and she would be on dry land. Dave noticed that the blade of the knife was slick with blood.

Lee was at the downstream corner of the wall, also holding a knife. He saw his father appear and yelled to him. "Melmoth, Dad!"

"Where?"

"Don't fucking know! Went under with the snakes, and when I came up he was gone. Never saw him at all!"

From where he stood, still backing toward the shallower side of the lake, Dave could no longer see any sign of the tangled nest of reptiles. They must have been lurking there, dozens of them, in the shelter of the partly submerged wall, and he'd blundered in among them.

Lee shrugged his shoulders at his father's question. The boy's face was quartz white with shock. "Down the river, I think. I killed one. Maybe two. But now Melmoth's gone...."

"Come out of the water, son," called Dave. "Toward me."

Shaking from the shock and the chill of the flood, they hugged each other once they were on dry land, on the uphill side of the huge pool.

"Can't we go and look for Melmoth downstream?" said Zera.

"No point. The cottonmouths must've gotten him and pulled him under."

"Oh, Dad, he was . . ." Lee was weeping. "A kind of symbol and . . . link with the old times."

"I know, Lee. It must've been real quick for him. Probably took several of them down with him."

Lee sniffed. "I guess he would. I'd have liked that, Dad."

IT WASN'T POSSIBLE to see it from far off on the mountainside, but much of Romero Springs had been destroyed by a catastrophic fire.

They had seen similar scenes in other towns. The surprising thing was that more damage hadn't been done at the time of the asteroid's colossal megaimpact with Earth. Gas lines had been ruptured and electrical shorts had triggered the conflagrations. So much time had passed that there was no possible way of knowing just what had happened in Romero Springs, but it had taken out a slice of the business section and most of the stores.

The shopping mall was a half mile north of the main residential area.

"If there's anything worth seeing, including Sheever, it'll be up there," said Dave.

Despite a temperature around twenty-five centigrade, the high relative humidity meant their clothes stubbornly refused to dry. Water seeped from their boots at every step.

"Can't we stop to build a fire and get ourselves dry?" Zera asked, running her fingers through her damp blond fringe.

"No. No chance. Could be Sheever's pushed off and is miles away. Could be he's about eight hundred yards away from us right now. That's why we have to try and keep out of a sight line from the mall. Any smoke showing and..." He allowed the sentence to trail away.

THEY FOUND fresh horse droppings in the center of Bachman Street.

Dave and Lee crouched over them, scanning the wet road for any clues. The boy backed away up the road and found an empty lot where half a dozen stores had been burned out.

"They cut across here," he called. "Looks like they don't have more than about nine or ten horses."

"Anyone on foot?'

Lee shook his head. "No, just horses. If we had Melmoth here, he could track them down for us."

Zera had walked a little farther up the street, then stopped and beckoned to the others.

"What is it?"

"Sheever's work, lover?"

On the left was an antique store, built into a small house. The fires that had ravaged Romero Springs had passed the building by. But someone else hadn't.

There were three corpses.

One had been an old man, as revealed by some white hair clinging to the head, and it had been male because the genitals remained. They'd been almost detached from the body, but they were still recognizably male. Nothing remained of the features as the entire face had been peeled away. One hand and leg had been mutilated, and a gash in the stomach was crowded by loops of pearly gray matter.

"God's plenty," muttered Dave.

The second corpse had been an old woman. This time most of the face was left. But the naked body had been strung up by the ankles to the supports of an iron garden swing to be used for target practice. The thick pool of black blood beneath it was attracting blowflies.

The third body was a teenage girl—probably the subject of a multiple rape, after which her throat had been slashed with such brutality that the whiteness of bone gleamed at the core of the dark-lipped wound.

Dave, Zera and Lee moved on in silence. Words failed them for a while, and they drifted through the town like dead leaves carried by the whim of the wind.

But they found several more dead.

"Looks like he cut a swath through the inhabitants of Romero Springs," Dave said.

"Some of these have died within the last few hours," Zera noticed. "They haven't been touched by birds or rats or anything. And the blood's still fresh and liquid."

"Why, Dad?"

Dave looked at his son, seeing the hurt in the dark eyes. "Always been some sick, mean bastards in the world, Lee. Sheever is...I guess he's just a man whose time has come, and he's relishing that to the full. That's why we're going to stop him."

PROGRESS WAS very slow.

A spectacular thunderstorm forced them to take cover in a ruined church. Most of its shingle roof had gone in the old fire but enough remained to give them shelter.

By the time the tempest had moved on toward the east, there were the first signs of evening gathering in the scarlet sky.

"Are we going on to the mall in the dark?" Lee asked. "It's an advantage."

"No. They still have enough men to post sentries. And we know some of them are military. Best recon the place first."

Zera yawned. "I'm tired. Wish we'd got something to eat. Can't we scavenge?"

Dave nodded. "Guess so. There's a number of possibilities about this place. Most of the folks could've run into the hills when Sheever arrived. Or he might have some prisoners, but I don't think that's likely. Can't see any real reason."

"Torture?" Lee said.

"I suppose that could . . . Or it might be that there simply aren't many survivors from the start of the long winter. It's kind of isolated up here."

"That could mean a chance of finding food around, couldn't it, lover?"

"It could. Let's go look."

They eventually struck lucky.

A side road wound up a canyon to the east, out of sight of the mall. The bottom had turned into a raging river, brown and frothing, but some of the neat houses along it were untouched.

They were obviously time-share apartments, used for odd weeks here and there by their owners. Some had been raided, but Lee found one that was virtually inviolate.

The door stood open, but nothing inside had been damaged. Dave's guess was that someone must have forced the lock, intending to return later. Then, for whatever reason, they'd never come back.

Zera went first to the bathroom and opened the mirrored cabinet. She whooped her delight. "Thanks, God," she said. "First time in months I've found any."

"What?" Lee asked, following her into the bathroom. He saw the packet she held in her hands. "Oh...those. Yeah. I know that..." He retreated, cheeks blushing, and bumped into Dave.

"What's Zera found?"

Lee shrugged. "Women's things, Dad. You know?"

Dave nearly smiled but didn't. "Sure, Lee. I know."

They looked everywhere. The cupboard in the tiny kitchen didn't hold anything more than emergency rations. Presumably they were meant for use if the owners turned up late at night with nothing else to eat.

"Not more stew!" Lee exclaimed.

"There's tuna," said Zera, shuffling cans on the shelves. "Eco-safe. And some of those self-heat Chinese and Thai meals. They're not bad."

Dave had been in the trim living room, investigating a walnut cocktail cabinet. "Not that I'm a drinking man," he said, carrying chinking bottles into the kitchen. "But I could easily force down a homemade piña colada and feel no pain."

In one of the closets they found terrycloth robes, and they all stripped off. The wet clothes were hung up in the hopes that they would dry out somewhat.

Zera dozed on a Naugahyde sofa while Lee opened some cans and Dave mixed piña coladas. There was white rum and tinned pineapple juice, unsweetened, sealed plastic pouches of condensed milk and a small can of cream of coconut.

"Shame we don't have any ice," he said, stirring the mixture around in a big pitcher with a view of Yosemite on its side.

Lee dipped a finger into the creamy liquid and licked it off. "Hey, that's double-good, Dad."

The pitcher didn't seem to last too long.

They sprawled on the thickly carpeted floor, relaxing in the pleasant buzz, mostly staying silent. Lee talked about missing Melmoth. Zera rambled on for a while about getting drunk in high school. Dave lay in the gathering darkness and sometimes slept.

During the night, probably a couple of hours past midnight, Dave came awake, thinking that he'd heard the sound of shooting not too far away. But it wasn't repeated, and he eventually wandered back into sleep.

He caught a vague memory of his mother tucking him into bed and reciting the same thing each night.

"Sleep well is what I say, tomorrow's going to be a busy day."

This time his mother was right.

It was a busy day!

18

Tuna fish with creamed corn and self-heats of instant sweet coffee were among the supplies in the cupboards. They tried self-heats of creamed oatmeal with added fiber, and all agreed that it was disgustingly inedible.

"Found some dog food here, Dad," Lee said. "Think we should take a can, just in case he manages to find us again?"

"I don't think we'll ever see the ugly brute again, Lee. But if we do, then I reckon we can do better than that dreck of sheep brains and cows' eyes."

"Caviar and venison?" said Zera.

"Maybe just the venison—and that reminds me. I meant to try and practice with the bow and arrows. Haven't used it in months. After it got soaked yesterday, I'm not sure it'll draw without breaking."

"I'll take it out back," Lee offered, "and try it for you."

"Sure. But draw it slow, and make sure you don't lose any of the arrows. We've only got a dozen and we might need those."

"We could make some more," said Zera.

Dave grinned. "Yeah. Full of tricks like that. One of the things you realize about civilization collapsing around you. Things you used to buy...drive down to Ken's Sporting Goods in Cody Heights... you can't get anymore. And the skills needed for an ordinary man to make his own arrows were lost two hundred years ago."

"We could have a shot at making them ourselves, Dad?"

"Course we could. And they'd eventually get to be about one quarter as good as what we've got now. If we get to live that long."

"I'll be careful with what we've got." He went out, closing the door behind him.

Zera looked at Dave. "When we finally go in against Sheever...are you taking Lee with us?"

Dave sat down on the sofa, nursing a can of mango juice. "Thought about that a lot. The simple fact is, when you've carried out the checks and balances, there isn't any choice at all. He has to come with me. Has to."

"With you, lover? Or with *us?*"

"Zera, you're a young woman and there's... I know life isn't what it was, but...but it's ahead of you. This isn't some pulp piece of fiction, Zera. This is real. Real fucking life, and there's going to be real fucking death at the end."

"I know all that, Dave, and..."

He waved a hand at her. "No, let me finish. In another day or so, if Sheever's around, this'll be done, one way or the other. And it won't be like the end of a book. Put it on the shelf and pick up another. There'll be corpses growing stiff, and they might be you or me or Lee or the girls."

She moved close to him and leaned down to kiss him on the lips, teasing him with the tip of her tongue for a moment. Then she straightened. "I guess that means that Lee is coming with us," she said.

THE PREVIOUS DAY, Sheever had been in a really good mood.

His man Angus had been a sergeant who'd been an expert on nuclear technology, and the man was working in the basement of the Paul Sheldon Shopping Mall. When Angus saw the power plant, he hadn't been very optimistic, but after a couple of hours he promised his leader that the mall would be self-sufficient by the following afternoon.

None of them dared make promises to Sheever unless they were dead certain that they would be able to keep them.

That had put the blond giant in high spirits, and he'd begun to talk about making the mall in Romero Springs his headquarters for the winter. He'd even gone into the toy section and picked out two dolls for the girls. A small baby for Roxanne, and for

Ellie a huge doll of a basketball player, complete with Lakers' singlet, shorts and long socks.

But that had been yesterday.

Now he was stalking the passages of the huge warren of a building, searching for one of his missing men. With only six remaining in his gang, every one was important.

"That fucking little prick. As soon as Jasper appears, I want to know. I'll break both his little fingers to remind him of duty and orders."

His only surviving lieutenant, whose background was Airborne weapons, was trying to calm him down. "Jasper probably went after the family that escaped us yesterday. We saw their house. One of them was that sports jock. Jasper likes young boys like that."

The grating voice of Sheever rode over him. "No, John. Think that, and fall into the same slimy tunnel as Jasper—am I kind and generous and easygoing? I have long dreamed of such a man, John. Old, surfeit swelled and profane. But I do mistake my person. I am not that man."

"I know that, Sheever."

The great head nodded slowly, and its shadow moved on the wall behind it, mimicking the gesture. "I know that you know, John. This can be a good place. A safe place. The people of this town were few and are now far, far fewer. They have barely touched the surface of the supplies held here. We have everything a man could desire. Everything. The great American consumer dream in Romero Springs. And it's ours. But we need every man to hold it. I want to see Jasper when he decides to honor us with his presence.''

"Sure, sir. Sure."

Sitting quietly in a corner of the atrium restaurant, the sisters watched Sheever and listened to every word. They both had their new presents with them. He'd be angry if they didn't.

And that wasn't a good idea.

"I DIDN'T TEST the bow, Dad," Lee said when he returned to their hiding house after a few minutes.

"Why?"

"It's in a bad way."

"Throw it away."

The boy shook his head. "No. If we keep it and then it dries out, there's a chance it might still pull and loose without snapping. But there are a couple of hairline cracks on it."

"Get rid of it, then. It's useless baggage."

"I'll carry it. Just for a couple of days or so."

Dave nodded. "Just two days. No longer."

They got themselves together and moved out of the apartment that had given them a chance to charge up their energies. They ended up on a road that simply wandered into the trees and then died.

The trouble with that was that they had to come out from cover and risk being seen from the dominating building above them.

Zera paused and looked behind, down into the partly burned ruins of the township. "The water is a whole lot higher," she said.

They all stared back, seeing that the small buildings near the entrance to the safari park were now almost completely submerged.

"Going to be something to see when the whole valley drains," said Lee.

"Any luck, and we'll be out of it." Dave looked up toward the mall. "Try and keep under cover as much as possible. There's no sign of any movement up there, but there aren't many outside windows."

In fact, it looked more like a military arsenal than a superstore. Its outside was paneled in black and silver, catching the morning sunlight. The huge parking lot, patterned with golden chevrons, was totally empty.

"I'm sure I just saw something moving, at the right side," Lee said.

"What? Man?"

"No. A horse...there!"

They all saw the animal, wandering on some grass at the flank of the mall. Even as they stared, a man darted from a side door and grabbed the horse by a dangling halter and led it out of sight, around the corner.

"Did he have a camouflage vest on?" Dave asked, rubbing his eyes.

"Yeah. Think so."

"So. . ." The word flat and final.

THEY REACHED another part of Romero Springs which showed some evidence of having been inhabited fairly recently. Among the evidence was a scattering of corpses. Most of them lay where they'd fallen, showing the multiple wounds from light machine guns. The body of a little boy lay alongside his three-wheeler, nearly ripped in half by a burst of automatic fire.

"None of them been mutilated," Zera observed. "Looks like it was done as a kind of exercise."

Though he didn't know it, Dave Rand instinctively made the right guess. "Bastard's culling the people. Picking out anyone left in town, so he can take it over himself and hole up here for the winter. This warm spell can't last, and that mall could be a great place." He paused, looking thoughtfully up at it. "Specially if he can get a generator going."

Less than five minutes after that, they heard the screaming.

At first it was just a noise. Far off, like a loose piece of metal scraping and squealing in the wind. Or a hawk, crying among the distant pines.

"It's human," Lee said, standing with his head to one side.

It was repeated, much louder and more desperate. Then the noise stopped abruptly.

They all looked at each other. Zera and Lee stared at Dave.

"What?" he said. "What do you want?"

Zera answered him. "The person screaming isn't one of Sheever's gang of thugs, is it, lover?"

"No."

"So, the..."

"Hell, I *know*. Let's go see, but for Christ's sake be careful. Guns out."

Around them the town was silent, but from way below, they could still hear the endless mumbling of the waters cutting through the valley toward the south.

"Came from over there," Lee guessed. He pointed to a narrow side road lined with secluded, single-story homes.

"Yeah. Best split up. Zera, take this side and keep on the edge of the sidewalk. There's trees for cover. I'll go around the back of the houses on this side. Lee, give me thirty seconds and follow me. If we draw blank, we'll turn around the far end and repeat it back to here.''

Dave was conscious that it was slightly colder than it had been. Some of the stifling humidity had eased, and the wind was fresh and clean.

The rear gardens were like any rear gardens in any small town. Some neat and some overgrown. Some orderly and some filled with discarded bottles and parts of old bicycles.

The Linebaugh weighed heavy in Dave's right hand, and he considered holstering it but decided against it. He walked on, his senses double-alert.

One more cry shrilled through the air, but it was quickly checked. Ragged and desperate.

It was from the next house along, or possibly the one beyond that.

Dave moved in fast, crouched, picking his way through piled domestic rubbish. A loose can shifted and rattled under his boots, but he ignored it. He stepped over a baseball bat with a heavily taped handle. The back door of the scruffy house was open, swinging very gently.

For a moment he considered finding Lee and using him as backup, but sometimes he still found it difficult to admit a need for help from his teenage son.

The hallway beyond the door was dark, with some light coming from a room at its far end. Dave began to cat-foot in, wincing as broken glass crunched under his boots, sounding deafening in the quiet.

There was a small kitchen on his right and a closet on the left, but he passed them by, drawn by the noise he could hear from the room at the end of the passage. Quiet moaning, almost like a kitten mewing with a thorn in its paw.

He hesitated in the doorway, then stepped quickly in, holding the heavy pistol in his right hand, bracing his wrist with his left hand against the demonic kick.

The drapes were pulled back, and the early-morning light showed him a slaughterhouse. A man and woman lay tangled in one corner, both dead.

The third figure was a young man, looking around eighteen. He was naked, and his superb muscular development spoke of dedicated bodybuilding. He was handcuffed over a stool, forced to bend in a contorted position.

Dave swallowed hard, barely managing to control himself, feeling bile rising in his throat.

The boy had been hideously tortured, his body a mass of wounds and burn marks.

Caked blood stuck to him everywhere, and only a feeble moan came from his lips. His life was at low ebb, and it seemed that he'd been left alive only to suffer to the inevitable end.

"Oh, Christ," Dave breathed.

The young man heard the whispered words and struggled to turn his head. The mouth moved, and sounds bubbled out of the broken lips frothing with bright blood.

The ghastly scene paralyzed Dave Rand, and he stood there for an eternity of timeless seconds, the Linebaugh forgotten, pointing at the floor.

He heard someone moving in the corridor, and he began to turn, expecting to see Lee.

It wasn't Lee.

Dave started to bring up the handgun, knowing it was too late. His mouth opened for a last scream of rage and despair.

The boom of the shot seemed to fill his ears.

19

He staggered backward, feet slipping in the lake of blood. There didn't seem to be any pain, no sense of crushing impact. Yet it was inconceivable that the man could have missed him at a range of less than twelve feet.

The back doorway was filled with the squat figure of his attacker, still gripping what looked like an Uzi machine pistol.

There was a second shot, and the man crumpled forward, falling facedown in the hallway.

Dave's mind began to work again, and he realized that he'd recognized the sound of the gun. It was the nickel-plated Ruger .32 that had once belonged to Janine and now belonged to—"Zera!" he called.

"You all right, lover?"

"Yeah." Quickly he headed for the rear door. He stooped over the wounded man, kicking the Uzi away from the open hand. Zera had actually shot him twice—once in the right shoulder and once in the middle of the back. He was still alive, turning his head and moaning with pain.

"What's inside?" Zera asked, but before Dave could say anything, Lee came running into the garden.

"Is Dad okay in there?"

"I'm fine, Lee. Stay out."

"They'll have heard the shooting up in the mall, Dad."

"Right."

Behind him Dave heard a feathering sigh from the teenage boy, and it triggered a blind rage in him. A ferocious red anger at the brutish inhumanity of Sheever and his followers. He pushed past Zera, brushing Lee aside with the palm of his hand, holstering the Linebaugh and looking around the yard.

"Dad . . . what are . . . ?"

Dave ignored his son. He turned his back and let out a yell of pain and rage, a long, drawn-out sound that came from the primal being at the core of man's soul. For a minute he stood still, his hands balled into fists, then calmly he went to the wounded man's side. Without a word, and with no more show of anger, Dave put a bullet through his brain.

Zera touched him on the arm. "What was that about?"

"Boy about Lee's age. This . . . this—" he pointed at the body "—this murdered his family and then tortured the boy."

"He's dead?" Lee asked.

"No. Not yet. But he's mutilated and beyond hope. Give me your gun, lover."

Zera handed him the warm Ruger without another word. She watched Dave as he stepped into the room at the far end of the corridor. There was a brief muttering that might have been a prayer, then a single shot.

"YOU SURE he was one of Sheever's men?" said Zera.

"Camouflage jacket. The Uzi. Sure."

"Why didn't you bring the gun, Dad?"

"Empty," he replied tersely.

That wasn't the truth. He'd never even checked the machine pistol where it lay blood slick in the opaque pool in the dark house. His rage had consumed all of his strategic sense, and he'd totally ignored what might have been a valuable addition to their armory.

They were moving fast up the hill, sticking to the eastern side of the valley and keeping most of Romero Springs to their left. The Paul Sheldon Shopping Mall hung above them, blank and faceless.

But there had been a sign of life.

Shortly after they left the house on the tree-lined road, they'd heard a loud, grating voice that bellowed down the hillside in a deafening shout. The actual words were distorted by the reverberating echo.

But they all agreed it sounded like someone calling a name that might have been "Casper" or "Jasper." It was the nearest they could get to it.

Dave squinted toward the mall, then looked back at Lee and Zera. "Let's get as close in as we can. Looks like there's a way through if we start from this side. Over that elevated parking lot."

Zera suddenly dived to the ground, pulling at Dave and Lee. She brought them down with her.

"Two men. Coming from the mall, both in camouflage jackets."

"On foot?"

"Yeah."

"Let's take them," Dave said. A tiny wave of regret flickered across his mind that they only had the handguns left. But it faded as quickly as the dew on a summer meadow.

The only thing that mattered was using the weapons at hand and their skill and determination to kill the two men who were moving blindly toward them.

IT WAS A GOOD DAY for Sheever. Angus had wisely kept his promise. The immensely powerful generator was humming in the basement, and the whole of the Paul Sheldon Shopping Mall had sprung into bright life. Elevators rose and fell, and moving staircases rolled. Recorded messages occasionally crackled out until a damaged tape disintegrated. Every corner of the mall was dazzlingly lit, and the air-conditioning struggled to clear the stale atmosphere and replace it with clean air.

Security locks on some of the main storage vaults, which had resisted previous attempts to force them open, now waited Sheever's ravaging.

"Going to be just like I said it would," he boasted, lying on a sumptuous four-poster with brocaded hangings. He was sipping from a cut-glass tumbler of Scotch.

"I sent Phil and Klaus out to track down Jasper and bring him in," said John.

Sheever peered at his lieutenant through the distorting facets of the crystal. "Good. Teach him a lesson—a tough lesson. Be cross like a devoted parent. You warned Klaus and Phil to look out for any survivors?"

"Yup, they got their orders. No mistaking that."

"This is, without a single shadow of a vestigial fucking doubt, going to be the life." He wrinkled his eyes. "John, where are our little precious princesses this morning?"

John's brow furrowed. "Think I saw them in the toys section."

"Think! You *think!*" His voice rose higher, like a circular saw speeding up through a sheet of plate glass.

"Yeah. I'll go find them."

As the man began to move, Sheever hurled first the glass and then the bottle after him. Both exploded into wicked splinters of jagged glass against the wall, missing the scurrying man by inches.

The good mood of the yellow-headed giant had vanished as quickly as it had appeared.

LEE COULDN'T STOP grinning nervously. "It's like games I played as a kid. Track and hunt, we called it."

Dave gripped his son by the shoulders. "I won't say that this isn't a game, son. I know you know that. But be careful!"

"Yeah, Dad. I'm deadly earnest."

KLAUS HAD BEEN a skilled thief in the army. He was short and pale, with the puffy eyes of the serious drinker. He carried an Uzi.

Phil was the oldest of the group, closing on fifty. His grizzled hair was cropped to the scalp, and he had the beginnings of a middle-aged gut hanging over his brass-buckled belt. There was a pump-action 10-gauge cradled in his large, capable hands.

They didn't anticipate any trouble from their colleague. Neither of them liked Jasper. As they trotted down into Romero Springs, Klaus spoke for both of them.

"Always the fucking way, man. Good friends gone down with bullets and knives or eaten alive by some parasites from the inside. Good, good men, right? And that murderous pansy comes out of it smelling of roses."

"Yeah. Bet we find he's been up to his usual stuff—disgusting as all get-out."

"Dead right you are man, dead right."

They were close enough for Dave, Zera and Lee to hear their voices.

Dave was behind the angle of a narrow, shaded alley to the right of the street. Zera stood just within the door of a looted jewelry store. Lee was a little farther down, inside a house, poised by an open window.

Now the voices were louder, and Dave, squinting around the corner, could see the men. One was armed with a machine pistol, the other carried a scattergun. Pump-action. Despite their military clothes, neither of them looked as though they were prepared for danger.

Dave flattened himself into the alley and let them stroll past before he stepped out, the Linebaugh braced and ready.

"Put the guns down!" he said sharply.

The two men froze, but both had fingers on triggers. They cautiously started to turn their heads toward the voice.

"Down now, or you're dead meat!"

But the one with the shotgun was still turning, looking at Dave over his shoulder and half smiling at what he saw.

"Just one, Klaus. With the biggest fucking Magnum you ever saw."

Now they were both looking at him, the muzzles of their weapons moving infinitesimally toward him. Dave breathed, slow and deep, knowing what he had to do and knowing he had to do it immediately.

He pulled the trigger on the gun, sending the .475 bullet rocketing along the eight-inch barrel and across the forty feet of space between him and Sheever's brace of killers.

At that range, at a motionless target, there was no way that Dave Rand could fail. He knew well enough that in a situation where there was any risk of a miss, the professional goes for the upper-chest shot.

At less than fifteen paces Dave could have put twenty from twenty through the center of a baseball.

Phil's head was a much bigger target, and the .475 blew it apart. It entered near the bridge of the nose and exited slightly to the left of the back of the skull.

It took out a whole chunk of bone matted with short, grizzled hair.

The man staggered back several tumbling steps, his arms out as if he were struggling for balance. The gun bounced down to the muddy earth, and he followed it, twitching for a few seconds and then lying still. The remainder of his brains soaked out into the dirt around him.

"Fuckin' hell!" said the other man. Apart from the fading echoes of the handgun's boom, the town was almost completely silent. He threw the Uzi down at his feet. "Don't shoot me, mister."

"How many men has Sheever got now?" Dave demanded.

"You live here?" asked Klaus.

"Just answer the fucking question and you might get to live a little longer."

"How many? Sheever himself. Plus John. And there's Angus the techno-man. And the two kids."

"Just three left?"

Zera's voice came from the far side of the street, making the man turn in surprise. "He's lying, Dave. Must be more."

Now Lee joined in, stepping into the street. "Could be true, Dad. The trail showed not many horses left and nobody on foot."

"It is true. That's why he wants to hole up here. Hold the mall. Got power for always, and more supplies than you'd fucking want for years. Got the girls, as well.''

"What do you mean about the girls?" called Lee, raising his 9 mm SIG-Sauer.

"Leave it," Dave snapped. "Time later for that."

Comprehension dawned in the swollen eyes. "Course—it's the girls. You're the fuckers who come after us all the fucking time."

Dave shot him through the face, putting him down alongside his dead comrade.

Neither Zera nor Lee said anything.

STANDING OUTSIDE the tall entrance doors ornamented in swirling art deco lettering, Sheever heard the shooting. Angus was still in the basement, happy among the polished generators. John was at the side of the huge man.

"Hear that?" Sheever said very quietly. "None of them had big handguns. Not Jasper, not Klaus, not Phil. Someone else."

"Who?"

Sheever slowly shook his head. "Soon find out. Let's go pretty the place up. Reckon we'll be getting visitors . . . very soon."

20

Sheever ran through the bedding department, passing the spot where he'd thrown the bottle and the tumbler at the wall. A tiny part of his mind registered the fact that someone had swept up the splinters of broken glass.

But he had far more important things on his mind and he immediately forgot it.

Roxanne and Ellie were sitting together in the department that had once sold children's books, reading quietly. Ellie had her anorexic basketball player doll at her side. One of its long white socks was missing.

"HE'S GOT all the cards, lover."

They were holding a council of war on the edge of the elevated section of the parking lot, looking down on the monolith of the shopping mall.

"Not so many. Time was he had two dozen trained men. Now there's him and a couple of others."

"Got the weapons."

"We've got the Uzi and a pump-action, as well as the handguns," Dave replied.

"And the bow," Lee said, taking it off his shoulders and drawing it in a threatening gesture toward the gleaming building. There was a dry crack, and the bow snapped clear across the middle, leaving the boy holding two halves linked by the string.

Despite the tenseness, both Zera and Dave rolled on the tarmac, barely containing their laughter at the look of stupefied amazement on Lee's face.

"I've carried this hundreds and hundreds of miles," Lee spluttered. "Now it breaks."

"Better now than when you're looking down the barrel of a light machine gun," said Dave.

After the interruption the three of them got back to their planning.

SECURE IN THE MALL, at least for a time, Sheever talked to his men. John was in favor of taking the horses and making a run for it after dark.

But Sheever was adamant. "No. We'll never find us a better place than this. And if we three can't hold off some piss-ant civilians . . ."

Angus was in his early thirties, with thinning hair. "I'm not that good with guns, Sheever. With machines, yes, but not with guns."

"You'll be fine." He looked around with satisfaction. "We got all the cards."

Sheever had moved his command base to the main vid-security control room. There was a whole bank of twenty screens, showing selected images from the two hundred small cameras mounted unobtrusively both inside and outside the mall.

Besides his last two gang members, Ellie and Roxanne were also there, sitting silently in the corner and watching the dancing, changing images: miles of silent aisles in the store; the illuminated fountain in the atrium; the acres of car parks, all totally deserted.

Roxanne suddenly straightened, her eyes wide. "It's Dad...and Lee..." She stopped as she realized what she'd done.

She'd stopped too late.

Sheever turned very slowly, his light violet eyes moving to the screen in front of the little girl and seeing the trio crouching among the bushes.

He smiled. "Dad," he said thoughtfully. "*Dad*. Now that does make things interesting, doesn't it?"

DAVE SAW the little gray boxes at every angle of the mall, their glittering lenses moving rhythmically backward and forward, up and down.

"Shit," he said quietly. "Never thought about the security cameras. The guy with the Uzi said they had the power on."

Lee looked up. "That means that Sheever can probably see us right now."

"Probably."

"Why don't—?" Zera began, but Dave stopped her.

"Quiet. I have to think about this one."

The spot where they were hiding was overlooked by the roof of the mall, and if Sheever managed to get any of his heavier weapons up there, he could sweep them away.

"Let's go," Dave said. He led them from the exposed part of the parking lot, running fast, feeling the muscles between his shoulders twitching with the expectation of a burst of lead.

ANGUS WAS GIVEN THE JOB of guarding the two girls.

"I'm going down in the atrium," Sheever said. "Me and John. Wait quiet and pick them off when they get inside. I don't want these kids warning them where we are. Take them up in one of the admin offices and hold them."

"Where will you be, boss?" asked Angus.

The sculpted head turned slowly, the eyes flicking over the girls in the corner and ignoring them. They weren't any part of any calculation.

"There's a row of phone booths under the balcony. We'll be in them."

"Sure thing. Want me to take the kids now?"

Sheever smiled at him with an infinite sweetness. "Why not wait until after the enemy get inside, Angus? Would that be a good idea? Or . . . might it just be marginally better to get the fuck out of here with them *now?*''

THEY WERE inside the mall.

Dave had guessed that Sheever, with his shrunken force, would probably choose to fight them on ground that he would know better. He'd wait somewhere and try to ambush them.

Since there were many side and rear emergency exits, Sheever couldn't hope to cover them all. That was his theory.

Now Zera, Lee and Dave crouched together in a service corridor. Dave had already checked the inner door, and it opened onto a row of small sales units. There were bright lights, and from somewhere they heard the faint sound of a fountain playing.

''Can't we split up, Dad?''

''No. Look, the logistics are simple. Three of them and three of us. He'll have hidden Ellie and Roxanne someplace, maybe with one to guard them. He'll not split up apart from that. So, if we split, we'll eventually face at least two to one. Three, possibly. If we're together and they hit us, there's still a fair hope we won't all get wasted at once.''

''But we don't hang together in a group?''

"Right, Zera. When I open the door, we go like I said. Me first, and you cover me. Then you and Lee. And watch and listen all the time."

ANGUS SAT in the huge leather swivel chair that had belonged to Pat Dickinson, once the manager of the Paul Sheldon Mall. He knew that because there was still a name tag on the dusty desk. In front of him was a console of flickering lights and switches controlling all the main security and intercom facilities.

He was holding his Uzi across his lap, watching the two girls who sat demurely on the sofa on the far side of the room. They were whispering together and occasionally giggling.

Knowing some of the things they'd been through with Sheever over the past months, Angus couldn't understand how the children remained so normal. They both wore faded jeans and parkas. Ellie's dark brown eyes would sometimes move to his face, and she'd smile. Roxanne didn't smile much.

"Angus?"

"What is it, Ellie?"

"Roxanne's got a tack stuck in the sole of her boot. Can she borrow your knife to get it out? Please."

The man was watching a screen on the desk, showing changing scenes from all over the huge complex. He'd spotted Sheever folding his seven-foot height into one of the telephone booths, with John moving into the second one from him. There still wasn't any sign of the attackers, though a light had turned from green to red, showing that an outer door had been opened in the last five minutes.

"My knife?" he repeated vaguely. "Sure. Don't break the point on it."

Roxanne caught it neatly and pressed the silver button on the black hilt, sending the blade clicking out. "Thank you, Angus," she said politely.

THE TENSION WAS agonizing.

Dave had visited plenty of big shopping malls in his life, but he'd never thought about the myriad ambush opportunities they offered. Every single unit had displays and counters and closets and fitting rooms, and Sheever could be behind any one of them.

Now he picked his way along one wing of the building, working inward toward the huge central atrium. He could glimpse it ahead of them, with trees and the silver glint of the fountain.

Lee was parallel with him on the left side, holding the Uzi. Zera was also on the left, a little behind the teenager, the pump-action shotgun in her hands. Dave had the Linebaugh drawn.

They passed store after store with merchandise ranging from designer sports shoes and unisex shirts to greeting cards, ethnic brooches, and wind chimes. A sweet smell surrounded a toiletries shop stocking soaps and perfumes, then they went past shelves and pyramids of paperback books.

It crossed Dave's mind that they were roaming the decks of an abandoned ship. Maybe Sheever had slipped away from one of the other exits and was heading cross-country by now.

The mall was a bright wonderland, filled with all the goods that had kept people longing for more and more of the luxuries of life, because there were few things to supply basic necessities in the mall. But all that was gone, wiped out. What really mattered to the survivors was food and warm clothes. Now the place seemed not like a part of ordinary life but something like heaven, something not quite real. It occurred to Dave, in a momentary lapse of concentration, that this would be a marvelous place to hole up after the girls had been rescued safely—close to a garden of Eden.

He caught himself and closed his eyes. "You prick!" he whispered to himself. "Think like that and we're dead. Focus on what we're doing. Focus."

They were getting close to the heart of the mall.

ANGUS SMILED. He'd been married once and had three children, though he hadn't seen them for years.

His daughter, Sharon, would be about the age of little Roxanne.

Now Roxanne was darting about the room, holding his knife in both hands, clasped to the top of her head, like a glittering horn.

He stood up to watch her better.

Ellie was encouraging her sister. "More, Roxie. You're the finest unicorn in the world."

Her little crouching runs were bringing her closer to the armed man.

SHEEVER WAS HOLDING an old Colt Commando, the XM-177 submachine gun. His finger sat lightly on the trigger as he crouched in the shelter of the phone booth, waiting patiently. The door was open just a slit, enabling him to see across the central area of the mall. He was smiling to himself at the thought that he would soon be emptying the 30-shot magazine and ending a pursuit that had become a major irritant to him.

A voice breathed through the stillness from his right, deeper in the shadows. "Coming," it said.

DAVE RAND PAUSED to wipe stinging drops of perspiration from his eyes. The atrium opened ahead of him, filled with bushes and trees, most of them pale and sickly. The fountain was chrome, lit from beneath, water cascading down its polished sides.

He took time to search the area with his eyes. His breath came slowly. "It's here," he said quietly.

This was where they were going to get hit. The prickling short hairs at the nape of his neck told him so.

It was a professional soldier's urban delight. A warren of heavy cover, with walkways and escalators and balconies. Endless dark nooks and crannies where an armed man might be hiding.

Lee and Zera were both looking across at him questioningly from their own places. He swept his hand in a brief arc, encompassing the space before them, and shrugged his shoulders.

The only way to go was forward.

He started to straighten, ready to step cautiously into the open.

"HEY, *TORO!*" Angus called with a chuckle, encouraging the stocky little figure as she weaved around him, the needle point of the knife held on top of her head.

They weren't bad kids at all. If he wasn't so scared of Sheever, he might've tried to help them somehow.

Ellie came close to Roxanne and coaxed, "Let me!" The younger girl passed over the knife, and Ellie started her whirling, flashing a teasing smile at Angus.

Roxanne had moved away, her eyes fixed on her sister's face. Then she tensed.

"Yes, Ellie," she said. "Now."

Angus was still smiling as she ran directly at him, hard and fast as she could, head lowered, the knife level with the top of his belt.

Only in the very last splintered second did Angus realize what was happening.

The blow was so devastating that he fell on his back, the girl on top of him. She was holding the knife in both hands, the blade sunk all the way into his body.

"Jesus...no..." were his last words as his life spilled from him in a red tide over the expensive broadloom carpet.

The last thing the man was aware of, apart from a shuddering coldness, was Ellie jumping over him, reaching for the switches on the console. He heard her beginning to shout something.

But by then a vast darkness started to surround him, and he heard nothing more.

DAVE STARTED to straighten, ready to step cautiously into the open when he heard his daughter's voice, deafeningly loud, cracked and distorted, but unmistakable. It came from every speaker in the mall.

"Dad! It's Ellie, Dad! Sheever and another one are in the phone booths under the balcony! Get them, Dad!"

All hell broke loose.

21

Despite having lightning-quick battle reflexes, Sheever was oddly slow to react. The girl's voice, so familiar to him, booming from the singing air all around totally confused him. A part of his brain accepted that Angus was probably dead, and another part recognized that his enemy was upon him *and* now knew where he was hiding.

That meant he was in danger of defeat, but that was unthinkable.

Sheever was never, ever defeated.

Lee was fastest to move. Hearing his sister's voice, he looked immediately beyond the fountain to the row of phone booths in the shadows under the second-floor balcony. He leveled the Uzi, already set on auto, and pulled the trigger.

The magazine emptied before he'd got halfway along the line, and the kick took the bullets higher and higher. Glass and plastic and metal exploded everywhere. A man burst out of one of the untouched booths, firing from the hip. Dave instantly saw that it wasn't Sheever, and he steadied himself, waiting for the giant to make his move.

His machine pistol empty, the teenager was fumbling for his pistol. John saw him and turned toward the helpless boy. Zera snapped off a round from the scattergun, but it went wide and high, smashing glass above the man's head.

Desperately Dave started to change his aim, and Sheever took that second to make his own move. The Linebaugh hesitated for a single, fatal moment.

John leveled his gun at Lee, ignoring his own imminent danger. Out of the corner of his eye he saw his boss diving into the darkness under an escalator.

The tableau froze. Zera was levering another round into the chamber. Lee was caught, his pistol halfway from its holster. Dave's gun was aiming nowhere.

Then there was a blur of movement and, his paws skidding on the smooth floor, coming out of nowhere, a brindled pit bull burst into snarling life. His jaws frothing, looking like a hound from hell, Melmoth was streaking toward the man threatening his young master.

John saw death racing at him, and he lowered his gun and fired a burst into the dog, kicking it over in a welter of blood and hair.

In that moment Dave had time to shoot John through the throat with the Linebaugh. The massive bullet nearly decapitated the man, snapping the neck and emptying his blood in one splattering torrent.

Before the corpse hit the floor, Lee was crouching over Melmoth, cradling the dog in his arms.

"You weren't dead and you—" his voice broke as he stroked the dog "—came back for me...." He turned to his father, tears glistening on his cheeks. "Melmoth's dead, Dad. This time really fucking dead."

"Time for this later, son," Dave said urgently. "Come on, right now!"

He led the way, crouch-running along the moving escalator. Sheever had gone up above them. He'd heard the pounding of his boots.

Zera was on his heels, and Lee a few yards behind her. Dave glanced over his shoulder. "He'll go for the girls," he said, his voice high and thin with the unbearable tension of the moment.

He was right.

There was a scream from the top floor, and he sprinted for it, emerging off the silent escalator, to finally face Sheever, man to man.

There was the slumped body of a little girl, blood around her swollen lips. Sheever stood almost astride her, one hand locked in the hair of an older girl who stood awkwardly, her right hand in her parka pocket.

The tall man had splinters of glass glistening in his long blond hair, and he held the Colt Commando casually in his right hand. The muzzle was jammed into the girl's neck.

"That's enough," he barked in his harsh voice.

"Hello, Ellie," Dave said.

"Hi, Dad."

"Roxie?"

"Sheever punched her out."

"Shut up," said the big man, setting the heel of his steel-toed combat boot on Roxanne's exposed throat.

Lee and Zera had fanned out on either side of Dave, and all three of them stood, guns leveled, waiting.

Dave spoke. "You've got my girls, Sheever. I've come a long way for them."

A croaking laugh came from Sheever. "Don't quote those fucking stupid heroic lines at me. If I had time, I'd tell you all about your late wife, Janine, and all about these two little dear ones here."

The Linebaugh lifted toward Sheever's face, but the man didn't move.

"Not even a fucking .475 cannon like that'll save them. Few pounds pressure, and the neck snaps. Tighten on the trigger, and her brains get to finish on the ceiling."

"And you're dead," said Dave, feeling utterly, totally helpless.

"Think that worries me? Not the going... it's the way of your going. Only the waste remains."

Everybody was frozen in place when Ellie made her move.

Her hand came out of the pocket, holding what looked to Dave like a white athletic sock. But its end was bunched as if something heavy was inside it.

Sheever wasn't ready for any resistance from the girl and made no attempt to dodge the attack.

All the months of loneliness, degradation, misery, humiliation and pain went into the blow.

The weighted sock swung up and around, hitting the tall man across the left side of his face, just below the eye. There was the distinct sound of flesh being struck.

Sheever let go of Ellie, shifting a couple of steps away from Roxanne's body. His hand went to his face, which was briefly reddened by the impact. Then they all saw a strange sight.

The cheek, slightly darkened, miraculously began to gush blood. It was as though the skin had been surgically removed, and crimson flooded out as if from a sponge.

The giant touched his face and looked at the dripping tips of his fingers. "Well...fuck me..." he said quietly.

Ellie swung her weapon a second time, and the packed splinters of broken glass inside it smashed directly into Sheever's left eye, pulping it in the socket. The white material of the sock was sodden with blood.

The big man dropped his gun, clutching his face, and he screamed once. The sound was piercingly, frighteningly loud.

Dave steadied the Linebaugh and shot him with careful precision through the mask of blood, the bullet striking the bridge of the nose. As Sheever tottered backward, Dave shot him three more times, each bullet pulverizing the blond skull.

The body crashed to the polished tiles and lay still.

Lee whistled softly. "Keying nice one, sis," he said.

"Thanks, bro," Ellie replied.

And then the tears began.

THEY DRAGGED the three corpses to the far side of the parking lot and rolled them down a grassy knoll, leaving them for the predators to remove. Melmoth was buried in one of the flower beds at the front of the mall.

The sun was setting across the mountains to the west, casting orange fire over the spreading lake that was swallowing Romero Springs. There was a fresh bite to the wind, promising a return to freezing weather.

They all stood together, Dave with his arms around his daughters. Roxanne's mouth was swollen and bruised from Sheever's attack. Lee was next to Ellie, and Zera close by on the other side of the younger girl.

Far above them there was a bald eagle, riding a thermal.

Dave spoke, his voice quiet and firm. "These are my children, that were lost and now are found. It'll soon be the New Year." He paused. "And a new life."

The Guardian Strikes

David North

A cloud of deadly gas is about to settle, and then a madman's dreams for a perfect society will be fulfilled. Behind it all is a sinister being searching for life-giving energy. He is the last of an ancient godlike race called the Guardians, and his survival hinges on the annihilation of the Earth's population.

Standing between him and survival are two men—the former CIA counterinsurgency specialist and the swordsman from the mists of time. Once again they join forces across time to defeat the savage being determined to destroy both their worlds.

Look for THE GUARDIAN STRIKES, Book 3 of the Gold Eagle miniseries TIME WARRIORS.

BEST OF THE BEST—AMERICA'S GIs IN WWII

CALIFORNIA

TIDE OF VICTORY
William Reed

Here's the gripping story of a brave handful of men who took back the Philippines. Exhausted by deadly combat against a ruthless enemy, Black Jack Company fights to break the back of the Japanese army.

The action-packed, authentic account of America's National Guard continues in BOOK 3 of SOLDIERS OF WAR.

Bolan is no stranger to the hellfire trail.

DON PENDLETON's

MACK BOLAN®

HARDLINE

Corrupt electronics tycoons are out to make a killing by selling ultrasecret military hardware to anyone with the cash. One of their targets is a man with one foot in the grave, an occult-obsessed defense contractor.

Mack Bolan finds himself enmeshed in a mission that grows more bizarre by the minute, involving spirits and Stealth, mystics and murderers.